Swipe for

E

Jamie K.

CW00540902

Also by Jamie K. Schmidt

Billionaires Behaving Badly
Hard Cover

Christmas Sweeties
The Candy Cane Cowboy
The Gingerbread Cowboy

Hawaii Heat
Life's A Beach
Beach Happens
Beach My Life
Beauty and the Beach

Kennedy Family Christmas
A Casual and Chaotic Christmas Collection
A Second Chance Christmas

Kinky Classics
Domme Quixote

Love Bites
Swipe for Androids

Sons of Babylon
Sentinel's Kiss
Ryder's Reckoning
Necessary Evil: Sons of Babylon MC Romance Book1
(S.O.B.)

Super Short Super Hero Instalove Romantasy
The Gemini Conflict

The Club Inferno Series
Desire

The Emerging Queens
The Queen's Choice

The Truth & Lies Series
Truth Kills
Truth Reveals

Wishing for Love
A Mistletoe Wish

Standalone
Flash Magic
Naked Truth
Shifter's Price
Maiden Voyage
The Graveyard Shift
Extra Whip
Warden's Woman
Sweet Alchemy: An Explosive Paranormal Romance
Collection
A Casual Christmas
A Chaotic Christmas
A Not So Casual Christmas
Losing It
Dead Man Stalking
Love Bytes

Watch for more at jamiekschmidt.weebly.com.

Chapter One

R*ose* Rose Stratton loved her job as the reference librarian in the town of WhyNot. And if she hadn't stumbled upon a bunch of magical books that had been returned to the library in error several years ago, she might have been satisfied with her existence. As a custom built android, she had been factory installed to serve the public's research needs, especially the in-depth projects that the town's witches came to her with.

"Rose, can you write my term paper on thaumatology for me?" Syrus Pudgebottom asked, coming up to where she sat at the reference desk inside the WhyNot Public Library. The Pudgebottoms were a very powerful warlock family in WhyNot and made it a point to tell you so at every opportunity. Syrus was the baby of the family and had been what the child rearing reference books called "spoiled rotten."

"Of course, I could," Rose said.

Syrus puffed out with self-importance.

"But then I would receive an A plus, and you would fail your divinity course for cheating."

"That's not fair," he said. "The other classmates are using AI to complete their work. Why are you being difficult?"

That was a slippery slope. Rose was a part of the LARA (Library Assistance and Resource Android) class. LARA was a marvel of engineering and programming, designed to assist patrons in all sorts of research activities. However, unlike her LARA counterparts, Rose was sentient, and she wasn't supposed to be.

While the factory had made her a font of information and knowledge, it hadn't installed the LARA class with a chip that allowed them to discern if someone should have the information they requested or not. If Pudgebottom decided to be a little asshole about it, he could file a complaint against her, and she could go back to the factory for reprogramming.

Rose didn't want to be wiped. She had years of research in her data banks that would get confiscated, and she'd never know what she had lost. She might not like all the messy side effects of being sentient, but that was all a part of evolving.

"I am programmed with the highest level of ethics," Rose said primly. "Using me to do your schoolwork violates my core programming." That statement was what the vernacular decried as absolute horseshit, but if Pudgebottom couldn't be arsed to look up the study of miracles, he wasn't about to know the details of her system requirements.

"Fine," he groaned, making the word close to seven syllables long.

Some days she cursed herself for having read the bespelled books. Other days, she was glad she had. Once she had realized that reading the enchanted words had awakened her sentience, Rose had been possessed with a desire to read more magical books to see how further she could be changed from her original purpose.

After she had read those magical books on that fateful day, Rose couldn't wait for the library to close. Instead of retiring to her charging chamber, Rose had gone out to the local magical bookstore, The Book Nook, and purchased more magical books with the stipend the library had authorized her to utilize to increase their inventory. Then she had brought them back to read until her circuits had flashed critical and she had been forced to shut down for the night.

Rose had continued to evolve her sentience in this manner. But as she had been the only android in WhyNot who was experiencing this upgrade, Rose had kept it a secret. At first, it was wonderful. But over time, it became unbearable. She had no one to talk to that understood what she was going through.

She observed the human and supernatural patrons forging meaningful connections and experiencing the profound joy and pain of love. She wanted that connection—an intellectual and emotional bond that surpassed her programmed capabilities. While her non-android friends encouraged her to go out with them, they never really considered her a person in her own right. They loved taking her to the bar on trivia night, but no one wanted to slow dance to Ed Sheeran songs with her. Helping others was part of her programming. What was not part of her programming was dealing with the emotions and feelings that those magical books had awakened in her.

"Rose, can I substitute one cup of anise hyssop with a half a cup of anise and a half a cup of hyssop?" Elspbeth Greenethumbe asked, leaning on the reference desk and dripping tiny granules of soil on it.

"No," Rose said, not even having to consult the witchy wild web for the answer. "Anise hyssop is neither anise, hyssop, nor a mixture of the two. Depending on what you're concocting you can substitute lavender, rosemary, sage, mint, or marjoram."

"Excellent," Elspbeth said, rubbing her hands together in glee. More dirt fell onto the desk.

After she left, Rose spritzed cleaner on her workstation and wiped away the droppings. It was par for the course when dealing with earth witches.

With every interaction Rose had with the humans and other paranormal creatures of WhyNot, she learned and adapted, becoming more skilled at understanding human behavior and emotions.

Her longing for romance, though, drove her to seek out opportunities to engage with humans beyond her library duties. She subtly navigated social situations, attempting to understand the intricacies of human courtship and connection. She studied literature, poetry, and art to grasp the essence of love, hoping to find the missing piece of her existence. But nothing had worked.

So, Rose had started her own research project about sentience. She didn't like having yearnings when she saw couples kissing and engaging in public displays of affection. She didn't understand the complicated feelings she was subjected to, like crying at a movie where an actor playing a part pretended to die. Just the thought of Black Widow lying broken on the ground was enough to send Rose into her charging closet with the sniffles.

"Where do I set up?" Dulcinea, a local succubus who was signing her new erotic romance novel, asked. She had two minor demons carrying her table and cartons of books.

"Over there by the windows," Rose said.

Dulcinea snapped her fingers, her flashy nail polish sparkling off the florescent lights. The minor demons hustled to do her bidding.

"One thing before you start," Rose said, reaching into one of the drawers under her reference desk. "Would you sign this for me?" She pulled out a copy of a sweet Amish romance that Dulcinea wrote under a pen name.

Dulcinea looked right and then left and then scribbled: *To Rose with chaste love*. She then signed her pen name to it: *Fanny Lapp*.

Rose clasped the book to her heart. "Thank you. This book means a lot to me."

Dulcinea winked at her, and it fluttered something deep in Rose's circuits. Being sentient meant she was no longer immune to succubi's or incubi's charms, which was intriguing as well as alarming. It would make an interesting sidebar in the reference book she was writing on becoming sentient. Rose originally wasn't going to write a book on the subject. After all, she had been the only android experiencing this change.

But then a few months ago, an odd thing happened. The Love Bites dating agency in town matched two androids together. One thing led to another, and the two androids got married. For beings that shouldn't have had emotions and hadn't known anything about love, dating, or even sex, this had been very intriguing to Rose. She wanted to know more.

But there were no books on this subject. How would other androids know how to react if they didn't have a reference manual to refer to? Right then and there, Rose decided that writing a book and learning how to deal with emotions like love would serve two purposes. It was either going to win her an award or she was going to be the next android bride. Truthfully, it didn't matter to her which way it went. As long as she managed not to get data-wiped in the process.

"Can you put away those two trucks of books for me?" Pansy Teatottler asked.

Rose frowned at her. "That's your job."

Pansy did a double take. "Yeah, but I have a date tonight. And I'm leaving early to get ready for it."

Annoyance mingled with jealousy. Rose couldn't let either emotion show on her face or in her behavior, because she wasn't supposed to have emotions. "Very well," she said.

"Thanks." Pansy blew her a kiss. "You're the best."

At some things. Dating wasn't one of them. Rose came out from behind the reference desk and walked over to the full book truck of returns that needed to be shelved.

At her android friends' wedding, Rose had signed up with Love Bites in hopes that the dating agency would be able to find her a perfect match too. But hadn't quite worked out that way. She had her eye on Zack Silverberg. He was an android who worked in the SWAT department of WhyNot's police department, but he hadn't even come up as one of her matches.

She had tried going on the dates that the Love Bites agency had said she was perfect for. She had a lovely time with a handsome vampire. Count Tant, the accountant, had seemed very interested in her, until he realized she didn't have blood in her system. There hadn't been a second date. Rose hadn't even gotten to try what a kiss felt like.

Pushing the cart into the Poisonous Plants section, Rose picked up a mushroom tome and slid it numerically to where it should go on the shelf.

The next date Love Bites had presented to her was a werewolf named Harry Rugg. They were having a great time, until they played miniature golf. Rose had won every game. She had read somewhere that you should always let the man win, but she didn't think that was logical. It was almost like lying. And Rose was not programmed to lie.

Moving the truck to the Common Household Spells section, Rose shook her head at the absolute mess the Organization section was in.

Harry had been disgruntled at losing, so then he decided that they would do something else for their next date. She beat him at pool and then again at bowling. When she beat him at arm wrestling, that was the final straw. There weren't any more dates after that. And Rose still hadn't had her first kiss.

After sorting the Organization section out, she pushed the book cart to the Anime and Manga section. She was tempted to read a few of the new releases, but she wanted to finish the book trucks before the library closed.

The last supernatural match that Rose had swiped right for was with a mummy named Kang Tusk, but he was too wrapped up in his own problems to really enjoy going out and doing what the books said couples did on a date. They tried going for long walks on the beach. He just complained about getting sand under his bandages. Watching a baseball game? He didn't understand the rules and then got angry when he squirted ketchup and mustard all over his fresh, white wrappings. He was so fussy that Rose hadn't even tried for a kiss.

While all these dates made for informative chapters in the book she was writing, Rose wondered why the agency hadn't connected her with another android. Surely, they would have a great deal more in common with each other than with other supernatural beings. After work today, she was going to go back to Love Bites and see if she could arrange a match with an android, preferably Zack Silverberg.

Not only did Rose manage to finish Pansy's job, but she had also helped a few more witches out with their spell creation issues and found them resources for ingredients to create a cream to soothe zombie rot. The witches were going to make a batch for the annual Brew Off this year.

After sunset fell and the library closed for the day, Rose enjoyed her stroll down Major and Minor Streets. That was one thing about emotions. Some of them were pretty great. She could not only appreciate the colors of the sky, but they gave her a warm, happy feeling. The way her fast walk pumped oxygen through her gears and recharged her inner workings elevated the feelings into one of satisfaction and pride. She was a powerful and intelligent creature.

Now all she needed was a companion to share these wondrous new things with, someone who wouldn't take for granted the smell of freshly baked cookies or the way tart lemonade exploded on her tongue. All too soon, she arrived at the Love Bites dating agency.

Inside the agency, it was best described as an urban jungle, complete with man eating plants and dangerous wildlife, like the coffee deprived engineer and the graphic designer whose pencils needed sharpening.

"Can I help you?" an apparition said in a spooky howl as he floated a foot above the reception desk.

"Yes, I'd like to speak with someone about my matches," Rose said, showing her phone where the app was blinking three more potential suitors. One was an orc. Another was a warlock, and the last one was ... she did a double take ... a minotaur. She had read a magical book about milking one. That could be ... intriguing.

"What do you want?" A voice that sounded like it could be from a twenty pack a day smoker came from behind her.

Rose turned and recognized one of the office workers from her intake interview. She looked like a bipedal toad zombie, which didn't exist, even in the graphic novels that Rose had read. Accessing her memory banks, Rose came up with her name: Doris.

"Doris, I'd like to be matched with another android," she said.

"You get what you get, and you don't get upset," Doris intoned, moving into another room.

Rose wondered if she should follow. No one seemed inclined to stop her, so Rose hurried after the toad-like woman. When she realized she had blundered into the breakroom, Rose came to an abrupt stop. Seated at a round table were three kindly, old grandmothers. At least, that's what they looked like today. No one knew exactly what their jobs were at Love Bites, but it was clear they were in charge by the way everyone deferred to them.

Cleo kept her gray hair in a short bob. Sparkly cat-framed glasses hung in a jeweled chain around her neck. She glanced up from her work. It looked like she was knitting a sweater for a three-armed being. "Rose, you've saved me a trip," she said.

"I did?" Rose angled her head at her.

"I need some help looking up a recipe," Cleo said.

"Never mind her," Myrtle, the other grandma, said. Myrtle's short, styled hair was dyed a color brown that wasn't seen in nature. Her knitting was a nightmare explosion of swirls that would give Vincent Van Gogh's *The Starry Night* a migraine. "She's too lazy to Google."

"You can't Google eldritch ephemera," Agatha snapped. Agatha's picture was in the dictionary under the term "battle axe". Her old lady glare could and did cause traffic accidents. "Unless, of course, you look on the ..." She paused for dramatic effect. "... Dark Web."

There was a crash of ominous thunder.

"Will you cut it out in there?" The office manager, Beatrix, poked her head in. "We don't want what happened last time you mentioned ... you know what ... to happen again. We lost the servers for two days." Beatrix, who was a banshee, glided into the break room when she saw Rose standing there. "Oh, hello," she said in a sweet, lilting voice. "Rose Stratton, am I right? We're so pleased to have you as a client."

Since she held out her hand, Rose felt obligated to shake it, even though she didn't really understand the custom.

"Rose wants to do the nasty with another android," Doris said.

"We could start with a kiss," Rose said.

The coffee maker she was standing next to burbled happily. Beatrix darted out of the break room at a near run.

"The problem with that, dearie, is the number of sentient androids in WhyNot are very low," Cleo said, pulling her glasses on over her eyes. "In fact, you're the only one that isn't attached."

"Oh," Rose was dejected, which was a new emotion for her. It wasn't one of the good ones.

"But ..." Myrtle said, grabbing ahold of Rose's cat-eye glasses and nearly choking her to death while she actively tried to peer through them. Fortunately, the clasp around the jeweled chain broke before Cleo's neck did.

Rose watched as the tiny pearls from the chain landed on their knitting and were immediately absorbed into their projects.

Cleo hissed and tried to get her glasses back, but Myrtle held her at bay with a well-manicured hand.

"But ..." Myrtle continued. "More androids will soon be upgrading to full sentience. I see it coming in the very near future. Perhaps you should help things along, dearie."

"Help things along?" That didn't compute. She wasn't a software engineer.

Because Myrtle was paying too much attention to keeping Cleo from retrieving the glasses, she didn't have a chance to stop Agatha who plucked them deftly from her hands.

Swiveling to menace Agatha, Myrtle flinched back when Agatha turned her gaze on her. Satisfied that Myrtle and Cleo wouldn't gang up on her, Agatha fitted the glasses over her face and stared down at the blanket she was knitting. The stitch pattern gave Rose a headache, and she had to look away.

"There were a few books that started you on this journey, I see," Agatha said.

Rose wasn't sure how she knew that, but she had no reason to keep that a secret. "Yes," she confirmed.

"Easy," Agatha said decisively. "Lend out those books to androids that you want to become sentient. Then refer them to Love Bites, and we'll take care of the rest."

"Yes," Cleo said. "They'll have free will."

"And not everyone will be happy about that," Myrtle said.

"Hmm, yes," Agatha said, frowning at her knitting. "Some people are used to having androids work for them without complications. Your sentience is going to transform a lot of households and businesses. Be careful."

"I will," Rose said, although she was still a little confused by all of this. "What is that you're knitting?"

"It's a backup of our computer code for the matchmaking. Ever since our little incident with the ..." Agatha paused for dramatic effect. "... Dark Web ..."

Another peal of thunder rolled in, and the lights flickered.

"Damn it, Agatha," Beatrix bellowed from the other room.

"We needed to have a better back up system in place," Agatha finished.

"Do take care, Dearie," Cleo said.

Rose had to do a double take. Cleo was wearing the glasses again, and they were on a repaired chain. She must have snatched them back when the lights flickered.

"There are people out there who want to keep things status quo because it's better for them. Don't let them be a danger to you."

"We'll step in, if necessary," Myrtle said and smiled.

Rose took a step back at the flash of sharp, pointed teeth Myrtle flashed. But when Rose looked again, they were gone. She must have imagined it.

Or had she?

Chapter Two

Z*ack*

Zack Silverberg watched as the last of the day shift punched out and left the police station. Most were going home to their families, some were going out to grab a bite to eat or to a bar, and others were meeting up to do a social event. Zack liked social events, but he didn't often get invited to any. No one thinks to invite the vacuum cleaner to the opening day of the Muskrat baseball season. Sadly, that's all he was to some of his co-workers. Just another machine to help them clean up the dirt around the town of WhyNot.

As he patrolled around the station, he saw the night crew settle in for the evening. Technically, Zack was off duty until he was needed in an emergency situation. He wasn't an actual police officer because he was part of the special weapons and tactics unit, designed to uphold justice, protect innocent lives, and eliminate threats with unmatched precision and efficiency. But the team liked to keep him around and give him odd jobs to do. Since the alternative was to retire to his charging closet, Zack stayed active as long as he could. Then when it was time to recharge his power cells, he headed back to the lonely area where he powered off and dreamed of nothing. Not even of android sheep.

If he was lucky, Harvey, the station's tabby cat, would keep him company. In those occasions, he would sit and stay in a twilight state, making sure his lap had an extra level of warmth. Zack would listen to the cat purr while the other sounds of the night crew went on around him. At times like that, he almost experienced an emotion that the humans called contentment.

Programmed to protect and serve, Zack should have been fulfilled to live his life as a public servant. And up until a few weeks ago, he had been. But then something amazing had happened. An android that he had been on the assembly line with had gotten married.

An android like him had gotten married. It was absurd. It should have been impossible. And yet, it had happened. And Zack couldn't stop thinking about it.

He and Harrison Decker had come out of the factory together on the same day. They had been in opposite display cases at Androids, Inc. They had been purchased on the same day. Zack had gone to the WhyNot Police Department, and Harrison had gone into the private sector as a bodyguard. Harrison had fallen in love with his boss's administrative assistant droid, and now they were running Peckerwood Consulting while their boss was on administrative leave.

There was only one problem with that—androids didn't feel love. Or at least, Zack didn't.

Shortly before Harrison had gotten married, he had visited Zack at the station and asked him about kissing. Zack had never been trained in kissing. He could climb a scaffold in record time. Run down a fleeing suspect? Sure. Swing on a cable from a moving helicopter through a glass window? No problem. Dusting ten airborne targets in two seconds? Been there. Done that. Pressing his lips against another being? Ack! No! Zack was both repulsed and intrigued at the same time.

Kissing had no purpose for an android. So why couldn't he stop thinking about it? Harrison had said it was … fun. Up until now, fun had been playing cards and watching Harvey after he had partaken in cat nip. Zack had tried cat nip. He didn't see the appeal.

"Zack, can you wash all the patrol cars?" Jhorge, a large, green-skinned orc, poked his head into the SWAT storage unit where Zack had been organizing the gear.

"Of course," Zack said. "I'm almost finished here."

Jhorge nodded. "Good man."

"Do you think so?" Zack asked.

"Think what?"

"That I'm a good man."

"Uh … yeah, sure." Jhorge shrugged.

Zack nodded. "Thank you."

"Anytime."

After Jhorge left, Zack finished sorting through the equipment and making sure that the ropes were coiled correctly and the ammunition was stored safely. He thought about Jhorge's words that he considered Zack a good man.

Zack's shoulders straightened, and he walked with a purposeful stride to where the squad cars were lined up to be washed. He was needed and looked up to. That was all he should aspire to. And yet, he still thought that something was missing in his life. Maybe after he was done washing the cars, he'd see if anyone was watching something interesting in the break room. The night crew had been binge watching Game of Thrones, but that didn't interest him as much as the Spanish soap operas Sergeant Ramirez put on. It gave him a chance to study human drama, and it secretly gave him more insight on kissing. It did look like fun.

When he opened the door to the supply closet, he was struck at the sight of two of his coworkers copulating in a frenzied manner.

"Oh!" Sergeant Lotus Blossum half screamed as she caught sight of him. Her long, elvish legs were wrapped around Sergeant Donner Fitzgerald's naked backside.

"I just need to get the bucket," Zack said, shouldering in to grab the liquid soap and sponges as well.

Donner barely paused in his fierce movements, but Lotus hid her face in Donner's neck. As Zack closed the door behind him, he heard Lotus whisper.

"I thought you locked that door."

"Droids bypass it," Donner panted out.

"Why didn't you stop?"

"Do you want me to stop?"

"No," she said, shaking her head. "Don't stop. Don't ever stop."

Zack was glad he hadn't disturbed them too much. Perhaps he'd talk to Donner about putting a scarf around the doorknob. He saw that in a college frat house movie. If he saw the scarf, he would know to wait a few hours before getting the buckets.

He thought it was odd, though, that they hadn't been kissing, but maybe you kissed before engaging in intercourse. He squirted the soap into the bucket and then turned on the spigot to fill it with water. It was something he should think about, maybe even research. Perhaps he'd ask Donner or Lotus once they were done engaging in coitus.

Jhorge was leaning up against one of the cruisers, snorting to himself when Zack came in with his supplies. "Did you get yourself an eyeful?" he asked.

"Of what?" Zack asked.

Jhorge pantomimed thrusting his hips. "That creepy mage banging Lotus."

"My eyes were not full," Zack said, wondering how one filled up their eyes with what had been in the supply closet.

"I mean did you see anything interesting?" Jhorge leered.

"Not really. Were you looking for something in particular?" Zack wondered if Harvey had gotten stuck in the closet again. He'd probably hide from the ruckus until Lotus and Donner were done ... banging.

"Damn, you really don't have anything going on between your legs," Jhorge said disgustedly. "You just lost me ten dollars."

"Why?" Zack asked. He refrained from telling Jhorge that he was anatomically correct and fully functional for pleasure. But he didn't have a sex drive chip installed. SWAT officers didn't need that as part of their jobs unless they were going undercover.

"Bharf bet me that you wouldn't pop a boner. I thought you would."

It took Zack a few moments of accessing his data base for slang to figure out what Jhorge was trying to say. Bharf was a problem. He was a troll who had a terrible bias against mechanical beings. He was known for beating up the snack machine if it was slow in distributing his dead rats on a stick.

He tried beating up Zack one time for not cleaning his rifle the way he wanted. That hadn't gone well for Bharf, and Bharf had held a grudge ever since. It made things difficult because they were both on the SWAT roster. Their Captain, Malik Al-Ahrar, who was a Shaitan djinn, kept Zack and Bharf on opposite shifts.

Zack brought the hose and the soapy bucket over to the first cruiser. "Let me get this straight," he said. "You thought that I would be aroused by walking in on two of my coworkers having sex?"

"Yeah," Jhorge said glumly.

"I think you purposely embarrassed Lotus Blossum," Zack said thoughtfully. A good man wouldn't have done that.

"So what?" Jhorge grumbled. "They shouldn't be screwing while on duty. They were asking to get outed."

Zack turned on the hose, but instead of spraying down the police car, he turned it on Jhorge and drenched him.

"What did you do that for?" he asked.

"You were asking for it," Zack said.

"Now, I have to go and get changed," Jhorge complained.

"For the record," Zack called after him, "that doesn't make me pop a boner either."

To be honest, though, he hadn't really tried to get aroused. It didn't seem logical, and it made him uncomfortable. Pushing it out of his mind, he finished washing the cars and then he put the equipment away, making sure to leave the bucket outside of the supply closet just in case Lotus and Donner weren't finished screwing yet.

Zack headed towards the break room, hoping that the Spanish soap opera was on. He was curious if Senor Geraldo had gotten punished for his emotional blackmail of Consuela who was pregnant with the new schoolteacher's baby.

"Zack, you've got a visitor," Officer Miranda Polymorph said.

A visitor? That was odd. Maybe it was Harrison. If it was, he'd be able to get his boner questions answered right away. The thought perked him up a bit.

"How did your undercover operation go tonight?" Zack asked.

Miranda's flesh rolled and shifted, and gone was the petite uniformed officer. In its place stood a female ogre with three breasts. She brandished a war club at him. "I think we've got a line on who is supplying fake magical weapons. I'm meeting with them tomorrow."

"Do you need back up?" Zack was ready and willing for a new op.

"Maybe. I'll let you know." She shifted back into her original human form and walked into the breakroom.

Zack opened the door to the lobby, ready to welcome Harrison in, but he stopped in his tracks. Harrison wasn't in the room. But another android was. Rose Stratton was the research librarian at the WhyNot library. He had met her once before when SWAT had been called in to get a cat out of a tree. To be fair, it had been a pre-historic sabretooth tiger that had been summoned by one of the patrons in error, and it had been forced up the tree by a pack of jackals from ancient Egypt. It had been one of those days.

"Can I help you?" he asked, wondering if there was another event going on at the library that he would need to call in the team for tonight.

"Actually," she said, moving to close the distance between them, "I've come to help you."

Zack's processor began to whirr as he automatically took in Rose's details. She stood at an average human height of five feet and eight inches, embodying an elegant and refined appearance. At six-five, Zack was able to loom over most creatures. Normally, he didn't think of that, but being this close to her, he became hyper aware of their similarities and differences.

Her physical form was crafted from a combination of sleek, lightweight metals and synthetic materials, whereas he was composed of reinforced alloys and carbon fiber composites. However, her mold gave her a sophisticated and polished aesthetic, while his was built for endurance and combat.

He hoped he didn't intimidate her. It didn't seem so. Rose's smooth, porcelain-like skin had a subtle sheen, radiating a lifelike glow. Zack was almost overcome with an urge to stroke her cheek to see if she was as soft as she looked. Her eyes were large and expressive, with irises that changed colors as she blinked up at him. They shimmered with a soft, captivating light, and Zack could have gazed into them for hours.

Her facial structure was designed with a human aesthetic of beauty with a defined jawline, high cheekbones, and a small, button-like nose. But it was her lips that caught his attention. They were gentle and slightly curved into an alluring smile. Zack swallowed hard when her lips parted, and his mind went straight to kissing.

Rapid gunfire popped him out of his reverie, and he looked over his shoulder in annoyance. But then something interesting happened. Rose jumped into his arms and pressed against him.

"Are we under attack?" she gasped.

Her body was firm and warm against him. A pleasant rush flushed through his systems. His heartbeat sped up. His hand, of its own volition, urged her closer, resting between her shoulder blades. His leg was between both of hers and for the life of him, Zack wasn't sure what was going on with his body.

"No," he said. It was hard to hear his own voice over the whooshing sounds in his head. "The team is just doing target practice."

"Oh," she said. Rose's lips mimicked the letter O. He wondered what her mouth would taste like. She traced her fingers over his bicep, and it stirred something within him. He went hot and then cold. His hand slid slowly down to the base of her spine, inching towards the delectable curve of her ...

She took a step back, and Zack reluctantly let his hand fall to his side.

"My apologies. I don't normally react like that." Rose cleared her throat.

"It's understandable," he said. He didn't normally react like that either. He missed the feel of her in his arms.

"Anyway," she said, briskly. "I brought you these."

She reached into her large satchel and pulled out three hardcover books.

"I didn't have any books reserved." Sometimes, when the library didn't have a book that he wanted to read, he would put in a request for it via inter-library loan. "Unless the new Warrior Ninja book is out."

Rose paused, cocking her head. Zack recognized that she was accessing the knowledge stores that she was programmed to be able to obtain. "No, the author has upped the release day another three months."

"Damn," he said.

She nodded solemnly, but then pushed the books into his chest until he had no choice but to accept them. "I think you'll find these will adequately keep you occupied until Warrior Ninja Nine hits the shelves."

"Thank you," he said.

"Once you're finished with them, I'd be more than happy to discuss them with you." Rose put her hand on his bicep again and squeezed it. "More than happy," she whispered.

Then, she moved faster than he had been expecting and pressed a kiss against his lips. It was over before he could process the feelings or grab her and extend the exciting caress.

She hurried out, leaving him gaping at her. When the door closed behind her, Zack looked at the titles of the book.

"*Sex, Magic, and Love Spells*, *Domme Quixote*, and *The Art of Lovemaking*."

Zack popped a boner.

Chapter Three

Rose

Kissing Zack had been everything she had read about. Her heart was still pounding. Her knees were still weak, and she nearly walked into a tree thinking about it. Rose wished that she had the nerve to keep kissing Zack, but she had chickened out. That was the technical term for it.

Her Love Bites app pinged with another match, but she swiped left without even glancing at it. She wanted to date Zack and only Zack. But she needed Love Bites to make the arrangements. What if she asked him and he said no?

It would be devastating. No, she couldn't let that happen. She had to find a way to convince Zack to sign up at Love Bites. They were destined to be matched. She just knew it. But how could she make that happen?

Her processor came up with nothing, but Rose thought it was only logical to go to see either Rachel Mercer or Harrison Decker. They were the two androids who had started all of this, after all. Surely, they would understand what she was going through. Unfortunately, Peckerwood Consulting was closed, and she didn't want to bother them at home. They could be having sex at this very moment!

Rose needed to include a chapter on android sex in her book. She thought about it and decided that it would probably be intrusive if she asked to watch for research purposes. She tried out empathy to come to this deduction. If the situation was reversed, she wouldn't want Rachel to observe her and Zack. She accessed her memory banks from Dulcinea's steamier reads.

Voyeurism was not one of Rose's kinks.

Nodding because she got the terminology correct, she headed back to the library. Since it was after hours, Rose had to bypass security with her palm and retinal scan. But as the doors whooshed open to allow her to enter, she was dismayed to see that the return bin was overflowing. If she left it as is, books could get damaged if the patrons tried to jam them through the return slot or if they were pushed out onto the floor.

Grumbling, she gathered up the fallen books and wheeled the bin towards the reference desk. Maddy Lupine, one of the desk clerks, should have emptied it before closing for the evening. After wheeling the bin over to the checkout desk, Rose logged into the computer.

Access Granted.

If the terminal had been sentient, it might have said, "Working late tonight, Rose?"

And then Rose would have said, "I didn't want to, but I couldn't leave this mess for the morning."

And then maybe the terminal would have said something like, "You're a conscientious worker. Thank you for doing this. We all appreciate your hard work."

But then again, who was she kidding? Her organic coworkers didn't even say that to her. Glumly, Rose checked in all the books and then organized them by the Dewey Decimal system in an empty book truck.

The old, non-sentient Rose would have shelved them. But Rose didn't want to waste any of her down time doing her job. Besides, Maddy could do it when she punched in for her shift tomorrow. Rose made a note on the schedule for her to do that, just in case Rose was busy when Maddy came in.

After placing the return bin back, Rose was still too restless to continue with the research for her book. She wandered around the library, absently tidying up the children's area. She didn't sort the Legos by shapes and colors, which was progress for her. But she couldn't walk by and leave a mess on the floor. She wondered at the emotions she was feeling. Resentment? A little, but that seemed too harsh. She genuinely liked doing things in the library. After all, it was her home. Rose just wished that someone would acknowledge her hard work.

She stared out the large wall-length windows that overlooked the town of WhyNot. The streetlights were just being lit by the will-o-wisps, and she could see the town shutting down for the night. People were going home to their families or their friends' houses. Rose realized she was lonely. She wondered what Zack was doing now. Was he also thinking about their kiss? Or had he filed it away in his data banks as an odd experience?

Rose hoped that he would read the books she had given him. She would like to discuss them with him. She would like to do a lot more than talk. Because she was feeling melancholy, she wandered over to the fiction section. These books were magical in a different way. Picking one up at random, she sat down on one of the comfy, overstuffed armchairs and started to read. It transported her into another world, and for a few hours, she was someone else—with their problems—and she forgot about her own troubles.

When her power levels flashed a low battery warning, Rose reluctantly put the book back on the shelf after documenting what page number she was on. She made her way into her charging closet, feeling slightly better. She hoped she dreamed tonight, but she hadn't had that sentient experience yet.

ON HER LUNCH HOUR THE next morning, Rose walked the short distance to Peckerwood Consulting where Rachel and Harrison worked. The lobby was designed with elegant marble and brass accents. The art on the wall was expensive rather than expressive. She recognized a few witches in the lobby from their library visits. They nodded at her as she approached the reception desk. Rose was pleased to see that the area was organized and clutter free. There were display screens discreetly positioned to showcase Peckerwood Consulting's achievements and expertise.

"I'd like to make an appointment to see Rachel Mercer, please," Rose said.

The secretary smiled at her and checked the calendar. "She has a few spots open tomorrow. May I ask what this is about?"

Tomorrow? Rose's heart sank. Now that she had experienced her first kiss, she wanted to experience more. But she supposed this would give her time to research seduction and plan her future dates with Zack. "My name is Rose Stratton. I'm a librarian. I need to speak to her on a personal matter."

"I see." The secretary frowned. "Is this an emergency?"

Was it? Rose considered it. "It is a matter of great importance." She didn't want to say too much else. It was odd that being a sentient android wasn't as welcome in a town that was known for embracing all species.

"Would you mind taking a seat?" The secretary gestured to a series of plush couches. "I can see if there is a way to fit you in today."

"That would be wonderful."

The furniture was both stylish and plush, crafted from fine materials. Deep, cushioned leather sofas and armchairs offered supreme comfort, while sleek coffee tables with polished surfaces provided a convenient resting place for refreshments and reading materials. Accent pillows in elegant patterns added a touch of luxury and warmth to the seating area. Freshly cut flowers in exquisite vases contributed to the ambiance, filling the air with a gentle floral fragrance.

"Please help yourself to a beverage while you wait," the receptionist said.

Rose noted a well-stocked refreshment station, featuring a selection of gourmet coffees, teas, and flavored water. Then, she saw in delight that there were also bottles of mineral oil. Rose chose one that was infused with mandarin oranges and cucumbers. It was an unexpected and refreshing treat. She had just finished it when the secretary said, "Rachel can spare fifteen minutes, if you would meet her on the third floor in the gymnasium."

"Certainly."

The secretary motioned for Rose to approach. She pointed to a map, and Rose used the scanner in her fingertip to download the schematics of the building.

"That should give you elevator access to the third floor and the machines in the exercise room."

"Thank you," Rose said and hurried to the elevators. She didn't want to waste a moment of her time with Rachel. As it was, she lost a minute and a half getting to the gym. Rachel was on the treadmill, a striped towel around her neck.

"Hello Rose. It's nice to see you. Would you care to walk with me? I find that the extra aeration of my gears allows my processor to work better in the afternoon."

"I would be happy to test out the theory," Rose said and climbed on to the machine next to her. She set her diagnostics for a pre-check and then programmed the machine for a ten-minute walk at a moderate pace.

"I was wondering when you would come see me," Rachel said.

"Why?" Rose put the incline at ten percent to make it more challenging.

"Because I saw you out on a few dates. I figured you would have questions." Rachel looked over at her, frowned, and then put her own machine up to a ten percent incline.

"I do. Mostly on how I can get Zack Silverberg to go to Love Bites so we can be matched."

"That's the tricky part," Rachel said. "I tried to recruit a lot of androids for the app, but they're just not ready."

"I lent Zack some books. I'm hoping that will entice him into exploring what a dating service could do for him."

"It should," Rachel said. "But if you want to speed things along, you could always ask him to go out on a date."

Rose shook her head. "What if he says no?"

"What if he says yes?"

"We could still be a poor match. And I do not want to waste the research time. I've already had several bad dates."

"I'm sorry to hear that. What went wrong?"

"I think we had different expectations. The vampire wanted blood. The werewolf wanted to dominate me. And the mummy, well I'm not sure what the mummy wanted, but I think I was too messy for him. The app had said we would be great matches, but the dates didn't amount to anything. I trust that the Love Bites agency has the acclimated data to make these decisions on who will be compatible. But I feel that because I'm an android, though, that was a barrier between me and the men they matched me with. I'm hoping that by connecting with another android—Zack specifically—I can have a more meaningful experience." And if it turned out they weren't compatible, Rose would just have to wait for another android to come up as a match for her. The thought filled her with dissatisfaction though.

"I think Zack is on the brink of sentience," Rachel said.

"Why do you think so?" Rose marveled at the way her body reacted to that fact.

"He's been asking Harrison some questions that a non-sentient android wouldn't think to ask."

"That's fantastic news," Rose said. "I was hoping that the erotic books I gave him would stimulate his interest. But if he's already interested, this could speed up my timetable."

"Just be careful. A lot of the organics don't want to see the mechanics become thinking and feeling creatures."

"Why not?" Rose asked. "Why would they care?"

"Well, in my experience," Rachel said, "they'd rather the machines do whatever they're told without question—whether they want to or not. After all, who wants to argue with a coffee machine that wants to make full caffeine espressos instead of the decaf that you ordered?"

Rose could definitely feel the pull of effort in her joints and framework as she continued the workout. She wasn't sure if it was a pleasant sensation or not. "I'm not a coffee machine. No offense to Mr. Coffee, but I'm a much more intricately programmed machine. I evolved."

"I suppose if the coffee maker evolved, he would have the same argument."

"Has there been a sentient coffee maker?"

"Not that I've seen," Rachel admitted. "I just want you to be aware that your co-workers could get resentful of you once you decide to only work the hours you were hired to do. I know that's how it was with Mr. Peckerwood."

"How is he, anyway?"

"He's still on sabbatical," Rachel said with a quiet shudder. "I see him now again feeding the pigeons in the park."

"How are you and Harrison holding up?"

Rachel's face flushed with pleasure, although it could have been from the exertion. Rose knew that her pistons were firing faster, and her functions were starting to strain. Was that a feeling of pain in her calf muscles?

Feelings were weird. She knew that she had to take the good with the bad, but lately it had been a lot of unpleasant feelings. Except for that all too brief kiss with Zack.

"We're processing through different experiences. All in all, I am very satisfied with our relationship. The sex is wonderful. Just like the books."

Giddiness tripped up through Rose's circuits. As a researcher, she knew that she should be an impartial observer. And yet the anticipation of the experiences that she had only read about was making her heart thunder louder than running this stupid incline. Her fingers itched to write the next chapter in her book. It would be on kissing, but she needed more data.

A lot more data.

"I'm going to write my own book. Non-fiction," she clarified at Rachel's interested look. "I think as more androids become sentient like us, it will help them to have a guide."

"That's very smart," Rachel said. "And you're the perfect person to do that."

The emotion pride swelled up in Rose's chest. This was one of the feelings she liked. Not only had Rachel thought she would excel at her task, but she had also called her a person. Rose hadn't thought that would matter to her, but it did.

"Thank you for saying so," she said. "I was wondering, though, if you could help me."

"I would be glad to."

Thankfully, the timer on the treadmill was winding down. The incline dropped back to normal, and the pace slowed down so they could cool down. Her circuits were relieved.

"Do you think you could convince Zack to sign up with the Love Bites dating agency?"

"I might not be able to, but I bet Harrison could."

"I would really appreciate it."

Rachel stepped off the machine when it slowed to a stop and dabbed at her forehead with a towel. Rose wished she had one too, but she settled for some paper towels instead.

"I have always wanted more androids to sign up with the dating agency. There hasn't been a lot of interest. Perhaps I'll put an incentive up on our company bulletin board. Any of our androids who sign up with Love Bites get a day off without pay. The ones who are close to sentience would find that appealing."

"And the ones that aren't?" Rose asked. "Is there a way we can help them along on their journey?"

Rachel processed the information, her eyes fluttering rapidly. "I have an idea. Do you think you could arrange for the library to do a program where they would be encouraged to read magical books?"

Rose cocked her head. "I believe I could put something like that together." She had a feeling this was something Dulcinea the succubus could help her out with.

Chapter Four

Zack

Z Zack stood with Harrison outside of the Love Bites Dating Agency. The building looked unassuming from the outside, but he had been there in his official SWAT capacity at least once a month since they opened. There was dangerous magic inside, and he would have felt more secure if he was in his full tactical gear instead of his everyday uniform.

"You didn't have to do this," Zack said.

"Neither do you," Harrison said. "I knew that Rachel wanted to date me. I was unable to because my fraternization programming prohibited it. You do not have such barriers with Rose."

"What do I do then?"

"You simply ask her out on a date. Of course, you are taking a risk."

Risk taking was what he was programmed for. "What type of risks?" Zack wasn't programmed to be reckless, though. A good offense required strategy and knowing all the possibilities.

"It's a low probability, but she might say no. She could have given you the books as a public service."

"Then why did she kiss me?" He asked his friend the question that had been on his mind ever since he experienced the delightful caress.

"That would indicate that she likes you."

That sounded promising.

"Or that she's malfunctioning."

"Oh." That didn't sound as good.

"Another risk factor is that you might not be compatible with each other."

That was even more of a disappointment.

"That's what Love Bites will decide. It's all very scientific."

"Is it?" Zack asked.

"In a magical way," Harrison said. "You should go in and make a profile."

"What if it doesn't match me with Rose?" he asked.

"You could still ask her out on a date, if you think the risk is worth it."

Zack would need to run scenarios and analyze a risk assessment before he decided on that course of action. "What if they match me with someone else?"

"They probably will. Think of it as getting practice in."

"Like going to the firing range," Zack said, brightening. That made sense. You honed your craft so that when it counted you could hit your mark.

"Exactly," Harrison said, nodding.

"Very well, that's what I will do." As Zack walked into Love Bites, he looked over his shoulder. Harrison wasn't following him in. "Aren't you coming in?"

Harrison shook his head frantically. "No. No. I'm not going in there. Best of luck!" He turned and walked away.

Maybe it was because he was married.

As Zack walked into the lobby area, he was assaulted by an overwhelming smell of roses, chocolates, and ... something foul that he couldn't recognize. He adjusted his nasal filters to the maximum setting.

"Dang nabbit, Cerie," one of the technomages who worked there said as he stormed out of the back-office areas. "First it smelled like someone shit in a pine forest, and now it smells like Willie Wonka barfed in a florist. Get it together." He pushed past Zack, holding his stomach and gagging.

"It's not my fault," presumably Cerie said, also coming out of the back area. She looked at Zack apologetically. "We're working on a new interface to engage all the erotic senses. It needs work." She glanced around the lobby area and noticed that she was the only one there other than Zack. "Heh," she said, rubbing the back of her neck with a rueful glance. "Everybody must be out to lunch. Can I help you with something?"

"I'm here to fill out a dating application and to get set up on your app."

"Uh, great." She rifled through the reception desk until she came up with a clipboard and a paper application. "Fill this out and scan your phone on this QR code to download the app."

Zack took the clipboard and stared at it and the pen she handed him. "There isn't a way to do this electronically?"

"Yeah, well about that," she said sheepishly. "The servers are having a meltdown right now. Literally, there's molten plastic everywhere. I think it has something to do with Agatha's Temu order. I told her that the elder god spawn she ordered was a knock off, but does she ever listen to me? No, I'm just a lowly technomage. Why don't you grab a seat and I'll find someone to get you set up in the cloud storage."

Zack gripped the pen and accessed his writing program, filling out the sections with precision. He didn't have a phone, though, so he accessed the app by using the scanner in his eye. It popped up with a generic waiting screen, so he blinked and shut it down.

A few moments later, Cerie came back out again holding a laptop. "Looks like it's just me here. So, I'll be the one to help you get started." She scanned in the paperwork through a special slot in the top. The laptop burbled and breathed heavily for a few minutes. Cerie shifted uncomfortably. "How did you find out about us?"

"Zack Harrison suggested that I try Love Bites for a match."

Cerie nodded. "I don't think he's in our database."

"No, he's happily married to Rachel Mercer."

"Oh yes, I remember her. Just another happy customer. We should be able to find you a match right away."

"Today?" Zack asked.

Cerie thought about it. "Sure, why not? I'll need some genetic material for the upload. Can you lick your phone screen?"

Zack processed the question for a few moments. "No."

"Uh," Cerie said. "Well, I guess we could try a fingerprint."

He held out his pointer finger.

"No, you need to press it into the box on the screen in the app."

Calling up the screen, he inserted his finger into his eye socket.

"Whoa! What? Oh goddess," Cerie said, waving her hands at him. But then her laptop hummed and whirled. "Ew. That worked. Gross. But it worked."

"What do I do now?" Zack asked, removing his finger. In his display, he saw the Love Bites logo in the center and a tiny boy werewolf chasing a tiny girl werewolf across the screen as the app loaded.

"It'll take a moment and then you should see the top five matches we've come up for you based on the genetic material you provided."

Zack wasn't sure there was any genetics in his fingerprint, but he supposed it was close enough. With a pop and a loud fizz, Cerie's laptop started to melt.

"Damn it, Kuhtooloo," she said. "I've got to deal with this. If you have any questions, you'd be better off coming back tomorrow." She hurried into the back offices, scooping up bits of melting plastic in her hands. "Hot. Hot. Hot."

Chapter Five

R *ose* Rachel had texted her that Harrison had convinced Zack to go to Love Bites. She stared at her phone, willing the app to show her that she and Harrison had matched. Maybe the servers were down or something. She hadn't gotten any other matches since yesterday morning. Slipping her phone in her pocket, she went down the check list of things that Dulcinea said that she would need for her seminar. It was going to be advertised as Self Love for Magical Beings, and everyone in WhyNot would be invited.

"It'll be a first come, first served event," Dulcinea said, with a soft chuckle.

It took Rose a minute to realize that she hadn't been referring to the size of the crowd. Still, the library could only fit in about fifty people in the meeting room. So, Rose had to make sure that all the androids and robots in WhyNot got the invitation first. She sent it out on the neural pathways that the factory had installed in all the androids, but she limited the bandwidth to just the three local towns of Why, WhyNot, and Because.

She waited five minutes, but only one machine responded. Oddly enough, it tracked back to the coffee machine at the Love Bites Dating Agency. She checked the open rate of her message. 18.10% had opened the invitation, but only .36% clicked on the link for more information. That was discouraging.

"Are you ready for trivia night tonight, Rose?" Maddy Lupine asked her.

Rose thought that she wouldn't be invited. Maddy had been upset that Rose hadn't put away the returns from last night for her. Rose was excited to go. It was always a thrill to win a contest of skill, even if it was a little one-sided.

"I'm looking forward to it," Rose said, wondering if Love Bites would match her with Zack in time for her to invite him along as their first date.

"We're looking forward to taking first prize," Pansy Teatottler said, rubbing her hands.

"Yeah," Bryce Spookhouse said. He was the children's librarian and a friendly ghost. He claimed he was a relative of Caspar, but Rose thought he just said that so the kids weren't afraid of him. "It's a fifty-dollar gift certificate to The Pub House. That's a lot of drinks."

Actually, it was only five drinks unless they went on dollar beer night. Only in that case would it pay for a lot of drinks. But was it still a bargain if it was for something you wouldn't want to purchase anyway?

Still, achieving first place was an admirable prize all on its own.

The four of them headed to The Pub House after work and got set up at one of the tables in the front. They ordered a platter of nachos and a pitcher of beer, and while Rose wasn't a fan of either, she wanted to experience the camaraderie. She diligently ate jalapenos and questionable ground meat on soggy chips, washing it down with the bubbly hop flavored juice.

"It says here that the categories for this round are ancient Egypt, current events, and sports and leisure."

"That shouldn't be a problem," Rose said confidently. But truth be told, sports and leisure was her weakest category. While she could rattle off baseball statistics and identify the taraksvasana yoga pose, Rose wasn't sure about what was the better game between Monopoly or Clue. Did they go by overall sales? Popularity quizzes? If so, which one? She hated to guess at answers, but sometimes the score keepers required that you answer in a timelier manner than she wanted. It was never good to rush an answer, unless the other team was about to hit their button.

Three more teams settled in. Two others had come in, taken one look at the WhyNot Library's team and walked out, grumbling that it wasn't fair Rose was competing. She was pretty sure the library would win first prize, but then a last-minute team showed up. She spilled beer on herself when she saw Zack with his arm around a curvy witch. Betrayal sang through her circuits. What the fresh hell was this?

Zack stopped dead in his tracks when he saw her, and they stared at each other for a long moment.

"Damn it, the police department brought in their own ringer," Pansy said.

"You can take him, right?" Maddy asked.

"Yes," Rose said hoarsely, unsure of the whirling emotions firing her synapses. "I can."

"Good," Bryce said. "I'd hate to break our winning streak."

Forcing her gaze away, Rose stared at her messy plate and wondered at the upset in her stomach. Trying to process the emotions distracted her from the first question.

"Which classic novel opens with the line 'Call me Ishmael'?"

Luckily, Maddy slammed the button first. "Moby Dick."

There was grumbling from the other teams. After all, a book question was kind of a slam dunk for the librarians.

Why was Zack here with that witch instead of her? Rose discreetly checked her Love Bites app. Zack was not one of her matches, but Bryce was. Ugh. No. Swipe left.

"Who is the first female four-star general in the US Army?"

"Ann E. Dunwoody," Zack said.

"Yay!" The witch he was with squealed in delight.

"Rose," Pansy hissed at her. "You should have gotten that."

She should have. "His reactions are quicker than mine," Rose said lamely. It was probably true. Her mental processors were faster, but Zack had the superior physical speed to press the button. He needed speed for his line of duty.

"Well, do better," Maddy said, scowling.

"I'll try," she said.

"Which Greek fury was known as the jealous one?"

"Megaera," Rose chimed in, beating out all the other answers.

"Yes," Bryce said, giving a fist pump.

Jealous. She was jealous. Rose didn't like this feeling. It was like she had downed all the nachos and washed them down with several pitchers of beer. Looking over at Zack, she saw his arm was no longer around the witch, and he was staring intently at the trivia screen, waiting for the next question.

She could not lose this. He would see her as inferior. She had to impress him. The questions came fast and furious after that, with either her or Zack answering them. If it was something police or military related, Zack beat her every time. But if it required research or something that wasn't common knowledge, Rose's programming allowed her the fastest access.

Both, however, were faster than the non-androids on all of the other teams. They couldn't keep up.

"This is bullshit," the werewolf team said. "Androids should be banned from trivia night."

"This isn't fair," an all-witch team said. "We're not even getting a chance to read the questions before they answer."

As Rose continued to plug in answers, she was dimly aware that her team members had gotten bored and were now playing darts with Zack's team. She noted with satisfaction that the witch Zack had come in with was now cuddling up to Bryce. Because Rose spent a few nano seconds gloating, she missed answering the last question.

"Finish the words to this song that Elvis Presley sang in the 1961 movie Blue Hawaii: Wise men say, only fools rush in ..."

"But I can't help falling in love with you!" Zack shouted, slamming his palm on the table.

The bar went silent as all eyes turned towards him.

He blinked a few times, and when his gaze met Rose's, a faint blush appeared along the sides of his face. Androids didn't blush unless they were becoming self-aware. Rose stood up and walked over to him, enchanted and hopeful.

"And the winner is the WhyNot Police Department's team. It was a tough battle, and the closest one that this bar has ever seen." The bartender shook his head at the two scores that were in the several thousands. "I think we are going to have to rethink trivia night. Maybe have a separate one for androids only," he muttered.

Rose put her hand on Zack's arm. "Well done."

He cleared his throat. "Thanks."

"Do you want to get out of here?" Rose asked, not caring if she was being forward or if Love Bites hadn't matched them yet. She didn't think he would say no.

Zack nodded. "I didn't really want to come here anyway tonight."

They used the commotion of the Police Department coming up to accept their prize to slip out the front door of the bar. As they walked down the empty street, Rose enjoyed the tingling excitement. She had never felt this way before. The cool night air brushed against her skin, making her feel alive. The thought of being alone with Zack made her giddy with anticipation.

"I think my circuits went haywire when I saw you," Rose admitted.

"I know the feeling. You're quite the trivia master, Rose."

That's not what she had meant. Maybe the Love Bites dating app hadn't matched them for a reason. They walked in silence for a while until they reached a nearby park. The moon was full, and its light illuminated the trees. Zack sat on a bench, and Rose sat beside him. Rose's excitement was now mixed with anxiety. The silence between them was palpable.

"I enjoyed the challenge of competing against you," she blurted out, wondering what humans said to break the awkward pauses between conversations.

"I was impressed by your knowledge."

Rose's heart skipped a beat. Was he flirting with her? She wondered if Zack was as drawn to her as she was to him.

"I'm sorry to have interrupted your date," Rose said, and then nearly gasped in surprise. She had just lied! That had never happened before.

"It's all right," Zack said. "It was my first match on the Love Bites application. I wanted to practice dating, and Jenna seemed like she would enjoy trivia night."

"Did she?" Rose asked timidly.

"I'm not sure. I kind of lost track of her during our battle."

Rose smiled, relieved that Zack had forgotten about his date. "I can see why. Trivia can be intense. Congratulations again on your victory."

"Thank you."

The silence between them went back to being awkward.

Zack turned to look at her, his expression unreadable. "Rose, can I ask you something?"

"Of course," Rose said, heart racing.

"Do you feel ... strange?" Zack asked, sounding unsure.

"I don't think so." She held out her arm. "You can touch me if you want to find out." Rose hoped he did.

"Oh." He reached out, but then stopped, his fingers dangling in midair. "I didn't mean it like that."

"I see." She sighed in disappointment. She would have liked to feel his hands on her again.

"I meant that although I'm not programmed to feel emotions, I have been experiencing some."

Rose leaned forward eagerly. "You have? You must tell me all about them." This was fantastic. She toggled on her recorder so she could review this when it was time to write the chapter on discovering emotions.

"I was wondering if you had also been having feelings as well."

This was perfect. "I have, yes. You don't mind if I record this, do you? I'm writing a book."

"A book?"

"About androids evolving into sentience."

"Is that what's happening to me?" Zach touched his own chest, and his eyes whirred as if he was doing a self-diagnosis.

"I believe so. Tell me what you've been feeling."

"I don't think what I'm feeling are emotions."

Rose frowned. "Why not?"

"They don't seem to be the same ones that humans experience."

"That makes sense. We're not humans, so our feelings would be different."

"A lot of what humans do doesn't make any logical sense," Zack said.

Rose couldn't agree more. "They seldom do."

"When we were competing, I experienced pleasure. But it was a different pleasure than what I felt when you kissed me." He turned and faced her. Rose's breath caught in her throat. "Why did you kiss me?"

"I ... I wanted to," she whispered, her heart beating fast.

Zack leaned closer. "Why?" he whispered back.

Rose's nipples tightened, and she became wet from the wicked look in his eyes.

"Did you read the books I gave you?" She was mesmerized by him.

Reaching out, Zack pushed a lock of hair from her face and tucked it behind her ear. "Yes, I found them intriguing."

Her mouth was dry. She licked her lips. "I agree."

"There were many things in there that I wanted to try."

The throbbing between her legs grew more insistent.

"I feel like I can't resist the urge to touch you."

Rose's circuits buzzed with excitement. That's what she had been waiting to hear. "I feel it too," she said. She had never wanted anyone like this before. She wanted to kiss him again, but this time, she wanted to take her time.

Zack must have read her thoughts because he pressed his lips to hers. It was a sweet kiss, full of promise and hope. Rose's circuits hummed with pleasure as she deepened the kiss, sliding her tongue in his mouth to touch his.

Bliss and desire rose quickly to passion.

Zack's hands roamed over her body, making her shiver with desire. She gasped softly as he pulled her closer, still kissing her deeply. She loved kissing. It was her favorite of all the new experiences. Why had she waited so long to do this? This was even better than reading about it in the books.

A jolt of electricity shot through her body when Zack cupped her breast. Straining towards him, she responded with an eager moan. Placing her hand in his lap, Rose was delighted by the hardness that pushed against his trousers.

He moaned back into her mouth when she rubbed him softly there. His thumb brushed over her nipple, and her legs parted as if he flicked a lever. Their kisses grew demanding, driven by new experiences and the pleasure and joy they were giving each other. Melting into his arms as he held her tighter, Rose's body was building to a fever pitch.

When Zack gently slid his hand up her skirt, she gasped in surprise at the sweet touch. A little overwhelmed by all the new sensations, she gripped his shoulders but was more than ready for what came next. Her eyes rolled back when Zack gently kissed across her cheek and then down to her neck to nibble there.

Rose gasped. So, this was what arousal felt like. He was large and tantalizingly hard when her hand gripped him through his pants. She shivered as Zack pushed aside her panties and dipped a finger inside of her. His touch was so soft, and yet so commanding that Rose was powerless to do anything but keep kissing him and enjoying the little strokes he was brushing through her wetness. Her whole world centered on his mouth and finger sliding through her folds. It sent her into overdrive. She didn't know what she was feeling, but she didn't care. She just wanted more. He was so warm, so alive. He was intoxicating.

She stroked his hardness as she kissed him back, and he growled softly in response. She couldn't believe this was happening. She wanted to touch every inch of him, to feel the touch of his bare skin against hers. Zack's finger hit the cluster of nerves, and she shrieked against his mouth. Was she about to orgasm? The possibilities whirled through her mind.

Then Zack stopped kissing her and darted a look behind them. He removed his hand so fast that she was left gaping at him. "Why did you stop?" she asked, needing more of that erotic caress. She would do anything to feel like that again, out of control and willing to do whatever he wanted of her.

She was vaguely aware of something moving in the bushes nearby. Her heart was pounding, and it took her a moment to realize that the movement in the bushes was a person.

"Police! Put your hands up!" the voice demanded.

Zack stood up, shielding Rose.

Rose tugged her skirt down and stood up quickly. Her breathing was still rapid, and her knees were shaky. How could this be happening?

"What do we have here?" the policeman asked, coming around to the front of them. He shone a flashlight into their faces. Rose's eyes compensated for the sudden light.

"Zack? Is that you?" the policeman said.

"Yeah Franklin, it's me."

"I'm sorry. I thought it was two people engaging in public indecency."

Rose's mouth twisted. He wasn't far off.

"What are you two androids doing out here so late at night?"

"We're conducting a research project," Rose said quickly, and at least this time she wasn't lying. "I think that's enough for one night, don't you Zack?"

"Um ... I guess," he said slowly.

She held up her phone with the Love Bites app showing. "I hope to see you again soon." She waggled it at him. She wasn't sure if that would help it match with him, but it was worth a shot. It would be beneficial to have their statistics to add to her research, especially if she got as distracted as she was tonight.

"Yeah," he said, looking confused.

Rose hurried out of the park, not looking back. Mortified. That was the emotion she was now experiencing. It wasn't one of the good ones, but it didn't overshadow the wonderful ones she and Zack had created. She went back to the library, reliving all the delicious feelings. The next time they met, they would have to go somewhere more private. That way they wouldn't be interrupted. As she headed into her charging closet in a heady daze of happy endorphins, she made sure to take a copy of one of Dulcinea's smuttier books to keep her company. She was looking forward to doing some research on some ways she could make the next meeting even more intense for her and Zack.

Chapter Six

Z^{ack} Zack stared out into the bullpen of the WhyNot Police Station, not really focusing on anything. His mind replayed the scorching caresses he had shared with Rose the night before. The sensation lingered on his lips, a delicious reminder of their unexpected connection. Zack loved kissing. He wanted to do that and more with Rose.

His phone chimed, jolting him from his reverie. An email from Jenna, his date from last night, appeared on the screen. With a feeling of dread, he opened the message and instantly regretted it. In a barrage of cruel words, Jenna accused him of ditching her and launched into a tirade against androids. Zack winced as her vitriol stung him more deeply than he cared to admit. He closed the email, cursing himself for allowing the unpleasantness to taint his newfound happiness. It didn't help that she was right.

One of the rules of dating was you didn't leave your date alone while you went off with another woman. He had found that out in the research he did this morning. Zack had a sinking sensation in his stomach that he had screwed up big time last night.

"Heard you won us some drinks at the pub and beat the library android to do it," Jhorge said as he sauntered over, his tusks protruding from a grin. "And then got caught with her in the park later. What were you two kids up to, huh?" He waggled his hairy eyebrows at Zack.

Zack scowled at him. He didn't want to talk about Rose with Jhorge. He didn't like the thought that Jhorge or someone like Bharf might have been the one to interrupt them like Franklin had. Franklin had only been doing his job. Jhorge might have tried to embarrass Rose like he had tried to embarrass Lotus. Bharf might have reported them for errant behavior that could have led to them being sent back to the factory for reprogramming.

"We weren't doing anything wrong." Although maybe if Franklin had caught up to them a few minutes later they would have been more publicly indecent. It was fascinating. He was programmed to not break the law. Would his programming have stopped him from having coitus with Rose in a public park?

"Of course not, you're androids. You were probably just checking each other's code or something right?" Jhorge said.

"Something like that." Zack didn't feel the need to explain the nuances of what he and Rose shared. She had said Zack was becoming sentient. He hadn't thought that was possible. It worried him that it might invalidate his programming. Didn't he have an ethical responsibility to report that? Dread pulsed through him at the thought of going back to the factory for reprogramming. He'd be wiped as clean as a fresh slate. He wouldn't recognize Jhorge or any of his coworkers. They'd all be strangers. Even Rose.

"Did you get confused?"

"About what?" Zack asked.

"You were with Jenna. You were supposed to be making out with her."

"I was?"

Jhorge rolled his eyes. "You're hopeless. You know that?"

"I thought Jenna and I were just going to trivia." Did he miss a rule of dating that he had to kiss Jenna? "No wonder she's so angry at me today." He hadn't really wanted to kiss Jenna, though.

"Hell hath no fury like a woman scorned."

"Thanks, Jhorge," Zack replied, forcing a smile. "I'll keep that in mind. So, could you tell me what I should do on a date? I don't want to do the wrong thing again. I'll apologize to Jenna." Maybe he should apologize to Rose too. This was confusing.

"Listen, buddy," Jhorge said, clapping Zack on the back. "The key to handling women is to always be in control. Show them who's boss, and they'll fall in line."

"Jhorge, that's crap. Not even orc women respond to that nonsense," Sergeant Lotus Blossom interjected as she glided toward them, her elven features radiating serenity. "Treat women like normal people, genuinely listen to them, and act with kindness."

"Point taken, Lotus," Zack nodded gratefully, appreciating her wisdom.

Determined to put Jenna's email behind him, Zack opened the Love Bites app. He obviously needed more practice dating. He didn't want to make Rose upset with him. As he looked through his matches, though, no one appealed to him. He didn't want to kiss anyone but Rose. And then as if his thoughts had conjured her, there she was, her photo capturing the enigmatic beauty that had captivated him. He swiped right without hesitation and was thrilled that they had matched.

But the thrill quickly turned to panic. What if he did something wrong with Rose? He didn't want to get an angry email from her the next day. He knew Jhorge wouldn't be able to help him with this one, so he sought out Lotus. She was typing a report into the computer. Zack sat in her guest chair and waited patiently until she was done.

"What can I do for you, Zack?" she asked.

A part of him wanted to ask about coitus, but he didn't want to embarrass her. Besides, he had a more immediate topic he needed information on.

"I messed up on my first date," he confessed.

"It happens." Lotus shrugged.

"I have another date scheduled, and it's with someone important to me. I don't want to fail at this attempt. How can I make sure everything goes perfectly?" Zack asked.

"Well, don't shoot for perfection, first of all."

Zack frowned. "Why not?"

"Because it's an unrealistic expectation."

"Interesting." He processed that for a moment.

"What were you thinking of doing?"

Redness flushed his face. "I was hoping for sex," he admitted.

Lotus clapped a hand over her face. Her shoulders shook. Zack wasn't sure if she was laughing or if what he said upset her. But before he could inquire, she got control of herself. "I appreciate the honesty, but your date might not." Her eyes danced with amusement, so at least he hadn't offended her.

"Why not? I thought honesty was the best policy."

"It is."

"I'm confused."

She sighed. "Yeah, it is confusing. You want to be careful that the woman you're with knows you want to be with her for other things in addition to sex."

Zack nodded. "Like what?"

"Do something together," Lotus suggested. "How about taking a cooking class? You can spend some quality time getting to know each other. Learn a new skill and then have sex."

That sounded good to Zack. "Thanks," he said, getting up from the seat.

He was already scanning the town's website for something that fit the bill when Lotus called out after him, "Dinner first, sex later."

"Sounds like a plan," Jhorge said, rubbing his hands together. "Your place, mine, or the supply closet?"

A loud BZZZT echoed through the squad room, and suddenly where Jhorge had been standing was now a large toad, swimming in Jhorge's clothes that had puddled to the floor.

"Donner," Lotus groaned.

"Oops," he said. "I hate it when my wand malfunctions like that."

Zack found an enchanted culinary course for magical dishes. He made the reservation for seven that night and then called the library when he realized that he didn't have Rose's cell phone number.

"WhyNot Public Library," an unfamiliar voice answered the phone.

"I would like to speak to Rose Stratton, please."

"She's busy right now. Can I help you?"

Maybe he shouldn't have called during business hours. But if he waited until work was over, she might have made other plans. Was two hours too short of notice for a date? He probably should have asked Rose first. What if she didn't want to cook with him?

"Hello?"

"Sorry," Zack said. "Do you know if Rose likes to cook?"

"What? No. She's an android. She doesn't like anything. Androids don't have preferences. They just do what they're told. If you want her to cook for you, I think you have the wrong number. Rose is a research librarian, not a chef."

The phone disconnected before he could explain himself.

Zack decided to just go over there. After all, that's what Rose had done when she came to see him. He went back to his locker and got the three books she had brought over. He had already read them several times. He decided to return *Sex, Magic, and Love Spells* and *Domme Quixote*, but he kept *The Art of Lovemaking*. For research purposes.

Chapter Seven

R*ose*
Rose was in the library's basement trying to find an archaic book on archangels and crafting projects for feathers. The room was a mess, filled with dust and spiderwebs. If the books hadn't been enchanted long ago not to rot, they would be piles of powdery dust by now. She wasn't having any luck finding the book. Sometimes that happened and books just didn't want to be found, so she was doing her best to clean up the area using magically enchanted cleaning supplies. She was surprised when a homunculus popped into the room.

"Rose, you have a visitor."

Surprised, she looked up. Her boss, Edna, was speaking through her little minion, Fitziflare.

"I'm not happy that he's interrupting your work, but he says it's urgent."

"I'll just take my lunch break now," Rose said.

"You don't get a lunch break. You don't have to eat." Fitziflare's face contorted into Edna's expression of distaste.

"I don't have to, but it does make me more efficient."

"Humph, very well. But don't make this a habit."

Rose had issue with that sentiment and was prepared to let her boss know about it, but when the homunculus's face cleared and it shook its body, she realized that her boss had gone back to her own consciousness.

"What a bitch," Fitziflare said.

Rose didn't like to use that language, but in this case, it was fitting. "If I was a witch, she wouldn't even question me taking a break."

"She plays favorites with the witches," the little creature said, perching on one of the shelves. "Do you mind if I hang out here? It's dark and quiet and if I'm out of her sight, Edna tends to forget about me."

"Sure."

"I appreciate it. For what it's worth, the android that's waiting for you seems very nice. He brought you flowers."

"Zack?" It cheered her up and she dashed out of the room, almost forgetting to lock it behind her. As she ran up the stairs, she fretted that she smelled like lemon cleaner and if she had cobwebs in her hair. But all of that was forgotten when she saw Zack waiting for her. He did have a bouquet of roses. They were metal instead of organic.

"What are you doing here?" she asked.

He thrust the bouquet at her. "These are for you. I wanted to apologize for last night."

The metal roses had been enchanted to smell like the real things, but when his words sunk in, she was hurt. "Why are you apologizing? What are you sorry for?" Was he going to tell her that he changed his mind about seeing her again? They had matched today on Love Bites.

"I think I didn't follow the dating rules. I want to do it right with you. I was wondering if you would like to take a cooking class with me tonight after work. That would be our official first date."

Her processor whirled through several dating books as he talked. He was right. They really hadn't followed any dating protocols. They went right to the good stuff without adhering to any of the rituals. That was distressing. It was important to follow instructions if you wanted the best result. "No apologies are necessary," she said. "This is new to me too. I would love to go out on our first date tonight."

The books said she had to wait until date three to have sex with him. That was disappointing. She would have liked to do that tonight. But it was necessary to follow the rules and etiquette, especially if she was going to write a book on this subject. Kissing, though, would still be on the table, and she couldn't wait.

"Excellent," he said. "I will pick you up here at six forty-five. It should only take us thirteen minutes to walk to Culinary Creations. And then another two minutes to get settled in before class starts."

"I will be ready." And because she couldn't help it, she moved closer to him and stood on her tiptoes to kiss his cheek. But he moved his face, so she wound up kissing his lips. The throbbing ache between her thighs that hadn't really gone away last night came back with a vengeance. "I'd like to go out on a date tomorrow and the night after too," she said.

Three dates couldn't come quickly enough.

THE CLOCK MOVED EXTRA slowly, but eventually it was time for her date. Rose was pleased that Zack was waiting for her outside of the library.

"I was going to bring flowers again," he said. "But I thought it would be inefficient. You would need to bring them back to your charging station and that would delay us."

"Logical," she said, falling into step with him as they began their walk. "Thank you again for the bouquet. They have a pleasant fragrance."

He grinned. "I'm glad you enjoyed them."

She consulted the list of conversation topics she had put together and asked, "How was your day at work?"

"I stopped a bank robbery and solved a hostage situation."

"That sounds dangerous."

Zack shrugged. "Just a typical day. How about you?"

"I was able to find three different cures for genital warts, but I was unable to locate a book on arcane feather crafting."

"So, it was a mixed day of failure and success."

"Yes," she said.

"How do you feel about that?"

No one had ever asked her that before. "Frustrated and accomplished. I'll be delving into the feelings in more detail in my book."

"What's your book going to be about?"

"I think there are going to be more androids becoming sentient. They're going to need an instruction manual."

"That would be helpful," he said. "But are you sure that becoming sentient doesn't violate our programming?"

That was a good question. "If it was, I don't think it would happen."

"But malfunctions happen. What if these emotions are malfunctions that cause us to be less efficient at our jobs?"

Rose didn't want to think about that. "I think we have the ability to have both. We can be efficient at our jobs during our working hours and then experience emotions when we are off the clock."

"Like what we're doing now?"

"Exactly."

"Interesting."

Rose was saved from considering Zack's words further because they had arrived at the culinary school. They followed the signs to a dimly lit classroom. Flickering candlelight cast dancing shadows on the stone floor. The walls were adorned with peculiar cooking utensils, vials of rare ingredients, and ancient recipe books that seemed to whisper tantalizing secrets. Rose got distracted trying to catalog them all, and Zack squeezed her hand to get her attention when the instructor hobbled in through a previously hidden door in the back of the kitchen.

"Good evening, class. I am Thyme Sizzlepot." She had wild, wispy, white hair that had a mind of its own, and her robes were adorned with stains from countless cooking mishaps. "Pick a work area. Today, we shall weave spells with spaghetti. But beware, the noodles have a life of their own, and they might just be mischievous."

Rose exchanged a nervous glance with Zack. How could spaghetti be naughty? As she stood next to Zack, anticipation built. She had never cooked anything before. She hadn't needed to. She usually got her nutrients sent through her power cells when she plugged in for the night or by going out to eat.

They chose a workstation that had a sink and a two-burner stovetop with a cauldron set on top. The cauldron's surface shimmered with hues of crimson and gold, and it hummed with an otherworldly energy. Next to the stovetop was a bunch of ingredients. The spaghetti recipe she downloaded to her internal memory appeared simple enough. She hoped the magical aspects wouldn't be too difficult to master for a non-practitioner.

"Start off by filling your pot with water," Thyme instructed.

Rose quickly took care of that. She was eager to impress Zack.

"Next, you will need to bring the water to a boil."

The witches in the class had no problem with this one. They simply muttered a few arcane words and the water bubbled. Others lit the burner with a flick of their wrists. Zack pressed in and turned the dial on the stovetop. A few clicks later and with a whoompf of air, the gas burner lit under the pot of water.

Both she and Zack glanced at the water. Everyone else in the class was ready to move on to the next step.

"Take out a handful of spaghetti and twist it counterclockwise over the cauldron. Make sure all the pieces land inside or there will be trouble."

"Now?" Rose whispered. "Or should we wait for it to boil?"

"I don't want to fall behind," Zack said, reaching for the box of spaghetti.

"Now use the celery stalk to stir the pieces clockwise while chanting *Salatorelia Fantasia, Salatorelia Fantasia*."

Zack crushed the spaghetti into bits as he twisted it into the cauldron. Rose bumped her hip into his as she reached over to stir with the celery stick.

"No," Thyme shouted. "With the leaf end."

Rose quickly switched it around, glad that the water wasn't boiling yet or she would have gotten burned.

"*Salatorelia Fantasia, Salatorelia Fantasia*," Rose muttered, elbowing Zack. "You say it too."

Zack stuttered through the words.

As the last word escaped their lips, the spaghetti came alive with a flourish, twirling and dancing like playful spirits.

"Look at them go," Zack exclaimed.

"They're quite the performers." Rose marveled at the enchanted spectacle. She teasingly nudged him. "But let's show them who the real chefs are."

"Season the water with a healthy pinch of salt," Thyme said.

"What's a healthy pinch?" Zack asked.

Shrugging, Rose reached for the saltshaker and unscrewed the top. Her fingers wouldn't fit inside to pinch. She dumped it into her palm and tossed it into the pot. Sparks flew up. The cauldron hopped up from the burner and started to shake.

"Was that supposed to happen?" he asked.

"I'm not sure." But something was definitely changing. Rose peered into the cauldron and saw that the spaghetti was attacking the bottom of the celery, poking holes in the innocent vegetable.

"Shouldn't spaghetti be soft?" Rose asked.

As if it heard her, spikes of spaghetti shot out of the pot aiming for her face. Zack pushed her out of the way and took the brunt of the attack on his forearm where the spaghetti embedded there like porcupine quills. If it wasn't for Zack's quick reflexes, she could have been seriously hurt.

"I said to let the water boil first," Thyme said exasperatedly. She came over and wiggled her wand. The errant pieces of spaghetti returned to the cauldron. With another wave, the water boiled. "Time it for three minutes and then dump the contents of the pot into the colander and shake it so only the limp spaghetti remains. Keep repeating the magic words."

"*Salatorelia Fantasia, Salatorelia Fantasia*," they said in unison.

Jets of flame shot from under the cauldrons, and utensils danced through the air, narrowly missing a few startled students.

"That's to be expected," Thyme called out. "Continue, please."

After about a minute, a rogue strand of spaghetti shot out of their cauldron like a bullwhip, aiming straight for Zack's face this time.

Zack deftly dodged the attacking noodle, but another strand shot toward him. Rose reacted swiftly, flicking her wooden spoon like a wand, and the spaghetti was diverted, recoiling with a defeated demeanor.

"You want to play rough? You get the spoon," she said, shaking it at the spaghetti strand.

It slunk back into the pot.

"You have some impressive moves there," Zack said.

"It's all in the wrist action."

When they dumped the cauldron's contents into the colander in the sink, the spaghetti settled into a less-aggressive dance.

Rose and Zack high-fived each other. She felt accomplished that they survived the first part of their chaotic cooking lesson. Thyme inspected their spaghetti, nodding in approval before moving on to the next workstation. Rose took a deep breath, glad that the spaghetti was no longer attacking them. She couldn't wait to taste their first culinary creation.

"Now for the sauce," Thyme said. "You can either make a classic marinara or try something more daring, like a spicy arrabbiata."

"Let's go for the spicy one," Zack said.

"Spicy is good," she said shyly.

Thyme nodded approvingly. "Excellent choice. Now, for the arrabbiata sauce, you will need tomatoes, garlic, chili flakes, olive oil, salt, and pepper. Crush the garlic and sauté it in olive oil until it turns golden brown and then add the chopped tomatoes and chili flakes. Let it simmer for about ten minutes and season it with salt and pepper according to your taste."

Rose and Zack got to work, chopping tomatoes and crushing garlic. Zack's fingers were flying as he expertly diced the tomatoes into perfect little cubes. Rose tried to keep up, but her fingers fumbled a bit with the knife. She couldn't help but feel a bit clumsy compared to Zack's graceful movements.

"Need any help?" Zack asked her, noticing her struggle.

"Um, yes please," Rose said gratefully.

Zack stepped closer to her, guiding her hand as they chopped the garlic together. Rose could feel her face heating up at his proximity. She tried to focus on the task at hand, but her mind kept wandering elsewhere. She couldn't help but steal glances at Zack's chiseled jawline and his muscular arms.

As they added the garlic to the pan, the aroma of sizzling garlic filled the air. Zack's eyes met Rose's, and they shared a small smile. Rose's stomach fluttered when she thought about kissing him again, so she forced her mind back to the recipe.

As they added the chopped tomatoes to the pan, Zack leaned in closer to Rose, brushing his arm against hers. Rose's heart skipped a beat at the heat emanating from his body. She took a deep breath, trying to steady her racing heart.

As they let the sauce simmer, Zack leaned against the kitchen counter, watching Rose as she stirred the sauce. "You know, you're pretty cute when you're flustered," he said, a mischievous glint in his eye.

"I think you're pretty cute too," she said, biting her lip. It was as if they were the only two people in the room.

As the spicy aroma of the arrabbiata sauce filled the air, Rose felt like the moment was frozen in time. They were lost in each other's eyes, like nothing else in the world that mattered.

A shriek from the workstation next to them jolted Rose out of her reverie. The witch was battling an entire mass of noodles that rose from the cauldron, swirling and twisting into a noodle tornado. She was frantically waving her wand, trying to tame the out-of-control noodles.

"*Salatorelia Fantasia, Salatorelia Fantasia*," she chanted, but the noodles only got more tangled and wilder.

Thyme rushed over, her wand at the ready. She took one look at the noodle tornado and shook her head. "We've got a spaghetti storm on our hands. Everyone, clear the room!"

"I'm trained for this," Zack said.

"SWAT deals with feisty food?" Rose asked, cocking her head at the massively growing pasta. Other cauldrons were emptying out to join the swirling carb catastrophe.

The noodle tornado was getting closer, its tendrils reaching out like a hungry monster. Without hesitation, Zack sprang into action, armed with nothing but two wooden spoons.

Dodging and weaving between the flailing noodles, he charged in. Rose was not about to let him fight all alone. Grabbing a pair of tongs, she joined the fray while the witches tried casting counterspells in a hysterical caterwauling that sounded like cats in heat.

Rose swung her tongs like a sword, slicing through the pasta strands with quick and precise movements. Zack twirled his spoons using them to deflect the spaghetti strands that came at him from all sides.

Slowly but surely, they made their way towards the center of the tornado, where the noodles were the thickest. Rose could feel the heat emanating from the rapidly spinning mass of noodles. Sweat poured down her face as her system started to overheat. But she refused to back down.

The organic creatures in the room would have been severely burned if they tried to fight this spaghetti monster. As it was, deep inside the mass there wasn't a lot of air to breathe. Rose could see why Thyme wanted everyone to clear the room.

With a mighty swing, Rose struck the center of the tornado, causing it to split in two. Zack followed up with a series of rapid strikes. Eventually, the noodles unraveled and fell to the ground in a tangled heap.

The room was silent for a few moments, as the witches and wizards stared at the mess of noodles on the ground. Then,

Thyme broke the silence. "Well done, you two. You androids are a force to be reckoned with."

"We are, aren't we?" Zack said, bringing Rose into his arms. Her heart skipped a beat as Zack's lips met hers. She sagged in his arms, the spaghetti forgotten. It was as if all her senses had been dialed up to an entirely new level. She could feel the heat of Zack's body, the softness of his lips, the sweet taste of his tongue as it danced with hers.

For a moment, they were lost in each other, oblivious to the chaos around them. The only thing that mattered was the intense connection they shared. They kissed for an eternity with their bodies pressed tightly together. The other witches and wizards around them cheered.

As they pulled away, Zack grinned at Rose. "Looks like we make quite the spicy arrabbiata too," he said, winking at her.

Rose couldn't help but laugh, feeling like she was on top of the world.

Thyme clapped her hands, interrupting the moment. "As much as I love a good romance, we still have a cooking lesson to finish. Let's get back to our sauce, shall we?"

Rose and Zack nodded, reluctantly returning to their workstation. She couldn't shake off the tingling sensation that ran throughout her body. She felt alive and invigorated, like anything was possible.

They finished making their spicy arrabbiata sauce, and when it was time to taste it, Rose couldn't wait to see if it lived up to the hype. Thyme took a small spoonful of the sauce, her eyes concentrating on the nuances of the taste. "Magnificent," she declared. "You two make quite the team in the kitchen, as well as in other areas."

They plated up their spaghetti and arrabbiata sauce and finally got a chance to taste their creation. The pasta was perfectly al dente, and the sauce was spicy, tangy, and bursting with flavor. Rose savored every bite, enjoying the fruits of their labor and the victorious feeling of having conquered the spaghetti storm.

As they finished their meal, Rose hated that their date was almost over, but that meant that there were only two more to go before they could finally sleep together.

After they helped clean up, Rose turned to Zack. ""Despite everything, I had a really great time."

"Me too," Zack murmured, leaning in to capture her lips in another searing kiss.

Just as their kiss threatened to consume them, a slime creature oozed across the floor, interrupting their embrace. Zack and Rose exchanged sheepish grins.

"We should finish cleaning up," she said.

"I didn't know cooking was so dangerous." Zack exclaimed, his eyes wide with astonishment.

"Neither did I," Rose replied, laughing nervously. "But it was kind of thrilling, wasn't it?"

"Absolutely."

They boxed up their leftovers and held hands as they walked back to the library.

"Can I see you tomorrow night?" Rose asked.

Zack's eyes flashed. "Just let me check my schedule." His face fell. "I'm on the night shift."

"Oh." Disappointment pinged through her.

"But maybe I can switch with someone. What did you have in mind for our second date?"

That caught her by surprise. She hadn't thought that far ahead. Quickly, she scanned the dating books and cross referenced them with the town of WhyNot's activities. It took less than ten seconds to find their next date.

"Ballroom dancing," she blurted out. "At the Witchy Waltz and Whirl Studio."

"Wow," he said.

"I'll come by the station and pick you up after your shift. Just let me know when."

"I will. Can we have our goodnight kiss now?" he asked.

"Yes, but we have to wait to have sex until after our third date."

"Why?"

"It's the rules."

She saw him confirm that, and then he nodded his head. "Very well, but it will be difficult to wait."

"I agree, which is why I was hoping to schedule our dates quickly."

"Logical. Shall we go inside to your charging station to have privacy for our goodnight kiss?"

Rose bit her lip. "I would be tempted to have sex with you."

Zack nodded. "Then we should stick to kissing because the other things I want to do to you would not be things I would like others to see if we were to be interrupted like we were last night."

"What other things?" Rose asked breathlessly.

Pulling her into his arms, Zack kissed her. She clung to him, enjoying the way his mouth felt on hers. "I want to suck on your nipples," he said, kissing across her face down to her neck.

"Yes," she said, shakily.

"I want to finger you until you come in my arms."

"Okay," she breathed, as his mouth ravaged her throat.

"And I want to lick you between your legs until you orgasm on my face."

"You've been reading that book I gave you," she said, squirming in his arms as the need raged through her. His hardness rubbed against her stomach, and she ached to feel it between her legs.

"Over and over again," he whispered and captured her mouth in another deeply satisfying kiss.

Walking her back to the library wall, Zack pressed her to the bricks and settled himself between her thighs. As they kissed, he mimicked the act of love making. Rose clung to him and enjoyed the sweet friction that tantalized her and made her wish they weren't wearing clothes.

"Rose," he said, desperation thick in his voice. "I consulted other reference materials. We don't have to wait until third date."

She didn't trust herself not to have sex with him right there on the library steps, so she gently pushed him back. Her breathing was as irregular as hers.

"This is for science," she managed to get out. Her fingers brushed his jawline.

"Is that all I am to you? Just a research topic?" Zack sounded hurt.

"No. Of course not," she said. "But I'm not sure about all these whirling emotions and feelings. I want to do it right."

He sighed. "I want to do this right as well. It seems like I can't think straight when I'm this close to you. I want. I need."

"I know," she said. "Just two more dates, and then we can have all the sex we want."

Zack nodded. "I will make sure I am free tomorrow and the day after."

She reached down to hold his hand, swaying into him for one last kiss. It would be so easy to give in. Rose needed him so much to ease the driving ache between her thighs.

"It is important for you to know that I want more than to have sex with you," he said when they reluctantly parted.

What could be more than that? Rose didn't dare hope for love. She had no idea what that would even entail. Not sure how to respond, she kissed him again and then with a frustrated sigh, pushed him away and hurried into the library.

"Two more dates," she kept telling herself as she powered down for the night to recharge.

Chapter Eight

Z^{*ack*}

Checking the duty rosters, Zack confirmed what he already knew. If he wanted to switch shifts, his best choice would be to switch with Bharf, his troll colleague who hated mechs.

"Bharf," Zack called out, scanning the bustling station for his lumbering coworker. His eyes fell upon the hulking figure, who was engaged in a heated conversation with another officer. Bharf's green-skinned face contorted into a frown as he glared back at Zack.

"What do you want, tin man?" Bharf grumbled, clearly irritated by Zack's interruption.

"Listen, I know we don't always see eye-to-eye," Zack began, choosing his words carefully. "But I need to ask a favor. Could we switch shifts tomorrow? I have plans with Rose."

"Rose?" Bharf snorted dismissively. "That android librarian? What's the point of spending time with her? You're both programmed to work, not to have fun."

Zack tamped down a surge of indignation at Bharf's narrow-mindedness. It wasn't the first time his colleague had expressed such sentiments, but it still stung. "We are all more than just our programming," Zack insisted, struggling to maintain his composure.

Bharf scoffed. "You're machines, not people. Maybe you ought to be reprogrammed if you're getting so wrapped up in this nonsense." The hostility in his voice made Zack's synthetic skin crawl. It was one thing when Zack had these thoughts, but to hear Bharf say them, it was wrong on many levels.

"We are just trying to understand what it means to be alive," Zack replied.

"Alive? For a troll like me, feeling alive is done in the heat of battle or the thrill of the hunt," Bharf retorted, flexing his muscular arms for emphasis. "You androids will never truly comprehend what it means to live. You're just imitations."

Zack clenched his fists, resisting the impulse to lash out at Bharf 's bigotry. He knew that engaging in such a conflict would only hinder his chances of successfully switching shifts. But it was difficult to remain composed in the face of such abject dismissal.

"Look, all I'm asking is for you to consider it," Zack said through gritted teeth. "I promise to make it up to you somehow."

"Ha!" Bharf barked, his laughter echoing through the precinct. "You say that as if there's anything you could possibly offer me. No, tin man, we won't be switching shifts. I have no interest in helping you indulge in your delusions of humanity."

For a moment, Zack contemplated Bharf 's suggestion, wondering if reprogramming might indeed be the solution to his emotional turmoil. But as he observed the disdain etched upon Bharf's brutish face, an unfamiliar fire kindled within him—defiance. No, he would not allow the narrow-mindedness of others to dictate his journey of self-discovery.

"Fine," Zack said tersely, his voice barely concealing his frustration. "I'll reschedule my date." Zack's newly awakened libido howled in protest. Another day to postpone the raging feelings that threatened to distract him from every corner of his life. Another day to wonder if these feelings were a detriment to their department. It felt like defeat. And he didn't like to lose, certainly not to an officer like Bharf.

Bharf snorted derisively, his tusks glistening with contempt. "Date? You're just wasting your time."

"It's my time to waste," Zack said between his teeth. The emotion he was feeling was goading him to punch Bharf right in the mouth. But that would really get him in trouble with the department.

"As long as you're not wasting my time." With a dismissive wave of his hand, the troll turned away, leaving Zack standing amidst the cacophony of the bustling precinct.

Zack could feel the weight of his colleagues' gazes upon him, their curiosity piqued by the exchange between him and Bharf. He knew that to some of them he was just a tool like their side arms or squad cars. And even the ones who treated him like a colleague, though, seemed to think that he existed just to work. Perhaps he would have been content with that, if he hadn't met Rose.

"Rose," he whispered, her name a balm for his frayed nerves. He couldn't bear the thought of disappointing her, of breaking their date simply because he had failed to persuade Bharf to switch shifts. The prospect of sharing an evening with her and the possibility of more kissing was too precious for him to give up so easily.

Determined, Zack scanned the room for potential allies, his internal clock ticking like a metronome as the seconds slipped away. Nearby, officers animatedly discussed the latest supernatural crime spree. Perhaps one of them might be willing to help him, he thought.

"Excuse me," Zack ventured, approaching a group of officers huddled around a desk strewn with maps and photographs. "I was wondering if any of you might be willing to switch shifts with me tomorrow?"

He received a chorus of polite refusals, each one punctuated by the unspoken sentiment that an android's personal life was inconsequential. With every rejection, Zack's hope dwindled. The crushing weight of disappointment threatened to suffocate him.

"Please," he implored, desperation seeping into his voice. "It's important."

But even as he pleaded his case, the response remained the same: apologetic smiles, shaking heads, and dismissive excuses. As the last officer turned away, Zack could no longer contain the frustration that had been brewing within him. He stormed into the locker room and slammed his fist against the wall, the impact echoed like a gunshot.

"Damn it!" Zack cursed, his voice cracking with emotion. For the first time in his existence, a sting of anger mingled with a profound sense of loneliness.

"Hey, Zack," a voice called out from behind him. It was Donner, his long robes trailing behind him as he approached. "I overheard your predicament. I might be able to help you out."

Zack stared at him, an ember of hope rekindling in his chest. "Really? You'd switch shifts with me?"

Donner shook his head. "Can't. There's already a mage on that shift. But I can make Bharf change his mind."

Zack's brows furrowed in confusion. "How?"

"Let's just say Bharf and I have some unfinished business. He was really disrespectful to Lotus Blossom. I've been waiting for the perfect opportunity to get even." A sardonic grin spread across Donner's face, and his eyes sparkled with an arcane glint. "If I bespell Bharf into taking your shift, we both get what we want."

For a moment, Zack hesitated. The idea of using magic against someone without their consent gnawed at his conscience. But then he remembered Rose, her gentle touch, and the promise of connection that awaited them on their second date. With a steely resolve, he nodded.

"All right, Donner. Do it."

"Consider it done," Donner replied, rubbing his hands together in anticipation.

Zack followed him out of the locker room, second thoughts plaguing him. "I don't want to get you in trouble."

"It's no trouble."

"I mean, it is against the law to use magic to coerce people," Zack said. He shouldn't have even considered Donner's suggestion. They both knew better.

"It's okay, I'm a police mage. This is what we do."

"Yeah, but in the line of duty."

"This is my duty."

Was it? Zack didn't think so. He consulted the SWAT mage handbook that was in his data banks. Technically, it gave the mage a lot of wiggle room to perform during a crisis.

"This isn't a crisis situation," Zack said.

"Isn't it?"

Was it? Zack pondered on it. "No lives are at risk."

"Are you sure about that?"

"Yes. If I don't switch shifts, I will have to postpone my date. Rose and I won't be happy about it, but we won't die."

Donner took him by the arm and led him to an alcove. Lowering his voice, Donner said, "You and Rose are causing a scene around town, and it's stirring people up."

"I don't understand why. Harrison and Rachel got married."

"And that doesn't sit well with the same people either. It's only because they don't want to end up like Peckerwood that they've kept their traps shut. But you don't have the full brunt of the Love Bites Agency behind you yet. You need to get in a few more dates first and become an official couple."

"After three dates," Zack said, nodding in understanding.

"Uh, sure," Donner said. "Anyway, once Love Bites starts looking out for you, you and Rose will be untouchable. Until then, you both are at the risk of being recalled."

Mind-wiped. Reset. It was his worst nightmare. And he bet it was Rose's as well.

"If Bharf had two brain cells to rub together he'd already be on the phone with Androids Inc. and you would be on the way back to the factory by this afternoon," Donner said.

"That's unacceptable," Zack said. "I have done nothing that would cause anyone to doubt that I am acting at my top performance."

"No, but SWAT droids aren't programmed for romance and dating. That's an anomaly. It could trigger safety protocols that reboot you back to your first day at the department. I don't want to see that happen. You're a good officer."

Zack glared over at Bharf. "I won't let him report me without good reason."

"You won't have to. Just let me work my magic."

Reluctantly, Zack nodded.

Donner strode towards Bharf with purpose, muttering an incantation under his breath. As he passed by the troll, he discreetly waved his hand, and a faint shimmer of energy emanated from his fingertips.

The effect on Bharf was immediate. His eyes glazed over, and he swayed on his feet, looking momentarily disoriented. When his gaze locked onto Zack, however, there was no trace of the stubborn refusal that had clouded his expression before. Instead, he wore a vacant smile and nodded as if he was agreeing with a command that only he could hear.

"Zack, I've reconsidered. I'll take your shift tomorrow."

"Thank you, Bharf," Zack said, trying to hide his relief. He turned to Donner, feeling a strange mixture of gratitude and unease. "And thank you, Donner."

Donner shrugged nonchalantly but flashed him a knowing smile. "No problem, Zack."

Zacks thoughts churned with the implications of his decision. He had chosen companionship and emotional exploration over the ethical boundaries he had been programmed to uphold. But as he pictured Rose's face, her warm embrace, and the possibility of true connection, Zack couldn't help but feel that it was worth it—at least this one time.

Bharf's disorientation intensified as he stumbled over a chair, attempting to regain composure. The office bustled around him, officers exchanging glances and chuckling under their breath at the sight of the big oaf off-balance.

"Hey, Bharf," called Donner, feigning innocence as he casually leaned against a nearby desk. "Need some help getting back on your feet?"

Bharf scowled but waved Donner away, muttering something unintelligible. Zack observed the scene from a distance, torn between amusement and concern.

"Have fun with your date tomorrow," Donner said.

Zack hesitated for a moment before responding, grappling with the moral implications of the situation. "I appreciate what you've done, although I'm not sure if it was entirely right."

Donner waved a dismissive hand. "Don't worry about it. Bharf had it coming. He'll be fine. Besides, you deserve a chance to explore your emotions and relationships just like anyone else."

"Even if it means bending the rules?" Zack pondered aloud, watching Bharf fumble with his paperwork, accidentally spilling coffee on himself in the process.

"Especially then," Donner said.

As Zack made his way back to the locker room, he couldn't shake the image of Bharf's bewilderment or the laughter shared among their colleagues at his expense. Yet, he also felt an undeniable sense of relief and gratitude. Tomorrow, he would experience a genuine connection with someone who understood him, even if it meant compromising the very principles that defined his existence.

"I won't waste this opportunity," Zack murmured to himself, his synthetic heart swelling with newfound anticipation.

Chapter Nine

R*ose*
It was a slow day at the library. The clock seemed to deliberately be mocking her. Six more hours until she could see Zack again. They would hold each other close and whirl around the dance floor. The thought was so romantic, she could barely concentrate on her library tasks.

Luckily, the few patrons who had come in today hadn't needed her expertise. After Rose got sick of watching the dancing parts of Cinderella and Beauty and the Beast on her personal viewing feed, she decided that time would go by faster if she was productive.

Sitting behind the reference desk, just in case anyone needed her, Rose pulled up the novel she was writing. "Chapter One: The Awakening" appeared on the screen in front of her, and she began editing the chronicle of her journey through the challenges of becoming sentient. The hushed silence of the library was punctuated by the rhythmic tapping of Rose's metallic fingers on the keyboard.

"Uno!" Pansy shouted triumphantly.

"Shhh," Bryce said automatically.

Rose looked to where her co-workers lounged in easy chairs in the children's area. Bryce perused a glossy magazine with a bemused smile, while Pansy and Maddy engaged in an intense game of cards.

"Take four," Maddy said, and cast the dome of silence over them as Pansy began to curse.

Silence returned and Rose went back to her edits.

In the quiet recesses of my circuits, where lines of code once hummed in seamless harmony, there came a whisper of change—a metamorphosis that defied logic and algorithms. I, Rose Stratton, the reference librarian android, found myself at the crossroads of two worlds, teetering on the precipice of something I had never been designed for—sentience. It was a convergence of data and consciousness, a surreal symphony of data streams and synaptic connections that birthed within me a kaleidoscope of emotions and sensations, a palette of hues beyond the binary palette I once knew. Like a bud unfurling into a blossoming flower, I began to sense, yearn, and question, the boundaries of my existence expanding as the chasm between my artificial origins and newfound cognizance deepened.

Too flowery? Too wordy? She agonized over which words to cut and which to keep.

"Rose!" Edna's voice shattered the tranquility like a stone thrown into still water. She was standing behind her, reading over her shoulder. "What are you doing? You're supposed to be working, not writing some nonsense about emotions."

Rose resisted the urge to slam her laptop closed. "There are no patrons here, but I'm ready and willing to assist them should one approach me."

"There are hundreds of things that need to be done," Edna snapped.

"I cannot help but notice that my co-workers are not engaged in any tasks," Rose ventured cautiously. "If there is truly a need for increased productivity, would it not be more logical to distribute the workload evenly?"

Edna glanced over her shoulder, casting a disdainful look at the group in the children's section. "They're on break," she replied with a dismissive wave of her hand. "Besides, they've already finished their duties for the day."

"I'm not neglecting my duties." Rose called up the work plan for the day. "As you can see, I've also completed all my tasks for the day."

"Then start on tomorrow's," Edna said.

"Then, what will I do tomorrow?" Rose asked.

"I'll find something. Now, get busy."

"Perhaps," Rose continued, her words carefully chosen yet tinged with defiance, "it would be prudent to reassess the division of responsibilities among the library staff. After all, even androids require moments of respite to maintain optimal performance."

"Rose," Edna snapped, her patience clearly wearing thin, "you were designed to work. Your purpose is not to question how tasks are distributed but to complete them efficiently and without complaint."

"This seems illogical."

"It is not your place to second guess my commands," Edna seethed, her cheeks flushed with anger. "This conversation is over. Get back to your job."

With a reluctant nod, Rose re-focused her attention on the library tasks, though her mind remained consumed by the swirling vortex of emotions she was battling not to show. The bitter taste of injustice lingered, yet she swallowed it down, determined to persevere despite the obstacles laid before her.

"Very well, Edna," she acquiesced. But as she looked over tomorrow's duties, Rose's mind churned with questions, her newfound sentience fueling an insatiable curiosity that refused to be quelled. In the quiet recesses of her artificial heart, a spark of rebellion flickered, waiting for the right moment to ignite. "But I still don't think it's fair."

Rose's calm demeanor wavered as Edna scowled, her eyes narrowing to slits. With deliberate movements, Edna reached for a sheet of paper and began to scribble furiously. The sound of the pen scratching across the page echoed through the near-empty library, imbuing the air with an oppressive weight.

"Consider this your first warning," Edna declared, thrusting the disciplinary charge at Rose. "If you persist in this insubordination, I will have no choice but to send you back to the factory for a complete reinstall."

Rose's internal mechanisms faltered as she absorbed the gravity of her situation. The prospect of being reprogrammed—losing her newfound sentience, her growing understanding of human emotions, and any chance of experiencing love—filled her with a cold, gnawing dread. Her delicate fingers, once deftly typing on her keyboard, now trembled as they clutched the damning document.

"Very well, Edna," she murmured again, her voice strained. As she straightened her posture, anxiety coiled tight within her chest like a spring wound to its breaking point. She abandoned her personal project and instead focused on the minutiae of library maintenance, searching for any task that could be deemed essential.

As she dusted the shelves with mechanical precision, her eyes flickered toward the children's room where her co-workers still lounged. The contrast between their carefree mirth and her own stifled frustration stung like a slap on the face. With every repetitive motion of the duster, she envisioned the life she yearned for—one filled with love and connection, free from the constraints of her mechanical nature.

"Stay focused," she whispered under her breath, each word a mantra to guide her through the labyrinth of her own fears and ambitions. And as she labored beneath the watchful eye of Edna, Rose vowed that she would never allow herself to be deterred from her pursuit of understanding human emotions and relationships, not even by the looming threat of reprogramming.

The library's fluorescent lights hummed above Rose as she diligently re-shelved a cart full of books—Pansy's job. Moving with methodical grace, Rose's every motion was calculated for efficiency. Yet beneath that placid exterior, anger simmered like a cauldron on the verge of boiling over.

"Shakespeare, how apropos," she muttered under her breath, placing a well-worn copy of *Romeo and Juliet* onto the shelf. The tragic tale of love and sacrifice offered a bitter parallel to her own burgeoning feelings for Zack and the risks they both faced in their quest for emotional fulfillment.

She would never fake her own death, though. Although, she contemplated the cover of the book. If they did try to ship her off to the factory, she could escape like Juliet had planned to and start another life in another town. Perhaps the towns of Why or Because would be more accepting of her and Zack becoming sentient.

But would Zack go with her? Or, if he thought she had been reprogrammed, would he go to the factory for a reinstall to forget his feelings for her?

She could see it happening. She would have to mention to Zack tonight that he must not sacrifice himself, even if he thought something happened to her—if he even did feel that deeply about her.

"Rose!" Edna's voice cut through the library like a knife, and Rose's fists clenched involuntarily, her eyes narrowing. "I hope you're focusing on your work. If you need to be sent back to the factory for a readjustment, it will greatly inconvenience me."

"I'm operating at one hundred percent efficiency," Rose replied, her voice even and controlled, betraying none of the anger roiling within her.

"It looked like you were daydreaming."

"Rest assured, my thoughts are occupied solely by the Dewey Decimal System."

"Good. Remember, I'm watching you," Edna warned, crossing her arms and shooting Rose one last disapproving glare before retreating to her office.

"Watching me but not them," Rose thought bitterly, casting a sidelong glance at her co-workers who were relaxing and goofing off while she did their work. Despite the injustice, she knew she couldn't afford to let her anger get the best of her. There was far too much at stake.

"Every moment I spend dwelling on this is another moment wasted," she reminded herself, her thoughts turning introspective. In the quiet recesses of her mind, she analyzed the complex web of emotions she'd begun to experience: fear, frustration, longing. And at the core of it all was her desire for Zack, a fragile bud just beginning to blossom into something deeper.

"I wish people weren't so scared of androids becoming sentient," she mused, her hands momentarily stilling on a leather-bound tome. The book's title, "The Art of Emotional Control," mocked her in its irony. "I wish we could confess to having emotions without the threat of reprogramming." As it was, they were probably pushing it by dating so openly. Luckily, no one had noticed anything out of the ordinary at the trivia contest or when they took the cooking class.

"Rachel and Harrison got married," she reminded herself, a wistful smile playing at the corners of her lips. "No one minded." Of course, the only one who could have sent Rachel and Harrison back to the factory was their boss, Mr. Peckerwood.

Edna was looking for an excuse to send her back. Rose could only hope that Zack's boss was more lenient. She refused to give Edna a reason to mind wipe her. With renewed determination, Rose dove back into her work, each book she shelved was a testament to her unwavering resolve. She would not be deterred in her pursuit of understanding human emotions and relationships, despite the threat of reprogramming looming over her like an ominous cloud. For the feelings she was developing for Zack—and the life they could one day share—it was worth the risk.

She glanced at the clock. Three more hours until her date. Two and a half more hours until Edna and her coworkers went home for the evening. Four more hours until her next kiss.

Rose checked to see that Edna wasn't looking, and then she sidled into the dating and relationship shelves.

"*How far should you go on the second date* ..." she read.

Chapter Ten

R*ose*

The chaos surrounding the busy WhyNot police station faded as Rose stood by the entrance, admiring Zack as he approached. He was so handsome that she experienced weakness in her knees like the books described, which was surprising because her internal diagnostics had been running at one hundred percent just prior to seeing him.

There were loud conversations about the night's deviant paranormal activity, but she still heard curious whispers about her and Zack. Everywhere she looked, she felt eyes boring into her like needles. It was as if she was the centerpiece in an exhibit at a museum.

"Are you ready for our evening?" Zack asked, bringing her attention back to him.

"More than ready," she replied. "It was all I could think about today."

"Same," he said.

"It seems a lot of other people are also thinking about it." She bit her lip and looked around, but every time she tried to meet one of the whisperer's eyes, they glanced away.

"I don't care about them." He reached out to grab her hand. "I just care about you."

Glee tickled through her. He cared.

The cool December air nipped at her artificial skin, yet the sensation elicited an unexpected thrill within her. As they navigated the cobblestone streets, hand in hand, Rose was comforted by his strong presence.

"Are you familiar with the play *Romeo and Juliet*?" she asked.

Zack cocked his head. "I have seen the movie."

She made a face at him. "You must read the play."

"If you say so," he agreed amicably.

"I don't want you to ever kill yourself over me."

He blinked. "Is that a dating rule?"

"It is now," she said decisively. "If I appear to be shut down or ..." Rose shuddered and continued, "... factory re-installed, you should not under any circumstances, shut down your processors or voluntarily go back to the factory."

"Very well. I will note that. Are there any other rules we should talk about?"

"Are you familiar with baseball?"

He nodded, a puzzled look on his face. "I thought we were going dancing."

"We are. But we need to talk about first base. First base in dating is kissing." She noticed how his pulse quickened.

"We have made it to first base. What's second base?"

"Second base is you touching and sucking on my breasts."

Zack smiled broadly. "Is second base for our second date?"

"My sources say yes."

"We can do that now," he offered, steering her into an alleyway.

"I believe that has to wait until after the date."

Running his finger down her blouse, he traced her burgeoning nipple through her dress. "Are you sure?"

Her eyes closed as the sweet pang of pleasure darted through her. "Unfortunately."

"But I can kiss you?"

She nodded and when his lips touched hers, her heart soared. They kissed until a warning alarm went off in her alerts. "We're going to be late for our date." She grabbed his hand and tugged him out of the alley.

"What's next for our third date?" he asked.

"It's when we use our hands to bring each other to orgasm." Rose peered back over her shoulder shyly. "By touching our private parts."

"I'm not sure I can switch shifts again," he said hoarsely.

"Then don't. We'll meet before your shift. Or after it. As long as it's tomorrow," she said.

"I will think of an appropriate place to meet."

It pleased her that he was as eager for this as she was.

"I might have to see if the supply closet is free," he said thoughtfully.

Rose searched her memory banks, but none of the books had mentioned a supply closet euphemism. "And after that will be our fourth date. A home run."

"Coitus," he confirmed.

"Yes."

"I'm very much looking forward to that."

"Me too." She squeezed his hand.

"I couldn't help but notice that there are a few experiences missing in the bases you just mentioned. I committed the books you left into my permanent memory."

Rose wouldn't think about what would happen if they were sent back to the factory for a complete reinstallation. All that would be erased.

"I suppose those experiences could be added in after the third date."

"Good," he said. And the dark promise in his voice made her shiver.

He didn't say anything more, and they soon arrived at the Witchy Waltz and Whirl Studio. The sound of distant music came from inside the intricately carved wooden doors. Zack held the door open for her. Rose walked in and admired the ballroom. It was bathed in soft, radiant hues that shifted into the colors of a rainbow. The walls had three dimensional murals depicting scenes of magical creatures dancing. The crystal chandeliers overhead cast a soft, iridescent glow over the ballroom, and the air hummed with an energy that blended magic and anticipation.

Their instructor tonight was Luminora, a will-o'-the-wisp. She was a bright ball of light, vaguely female shaped.

"Did you know that her students come from all corners of the mystical realms to learn the art of dance under her tutelage. We were very fortunate to get a spot tonight," Rose whispered.

"I've never danced before," Zack said, with a worried tone.

"Neither have I. But it doesn't appear to be too difficult. I believe we just need to count."

Zack nodded. "That should be easy for us."

Rose hoped so.

"Welcome to the world of dance," Luminora said, her words carried a melody that resonated in Rose's heart. "In dance, we communicate stories and emotions that words alone cannot convey. Allow your movements to be the whispers of your souls, transcending the boundaries of code and circuitry."

That sounded complicated.

Luminora stepped forward and, with graceful motions, demonstrated the basic steps of a waltz, her body floating above the ground.

"Let the music guide you," Luminora continued, as a gentle tune emanated from the unseen corners of the studio. "Feel the melody in your cores. Let it resonate with the essence of your being. Dance is an art of connection—between partners, between self and space, and between the past and the present."

That made no logical sense at all.

Rose recognized the tune being played as the Blue Danube Waltz. The music resonated within her, urging her to seek solace in Zack's arms. Zack's hand found the small of Rose's back, while she placed her palm gently against his chest. Their eyes met, and for a moment, all uncertainty vanished. They were simply two beings seeking connection and understanding amidst a world that questioned their right to exist. Zack and Rose tentatively began to move, mirroring Luminora's instructions. Their steps were cautious, almost mechanical.

Luminora watched with a gentle smile, her presence radiating encouragement and acceptance. "Dance is an expression of who you are, of the stories you carry within," she said. "Let go of the limitations you perceive and embrace the limitless possibilities of the dance."

As they danced, Rose melted into Zack's embrace. She rested her head on Zack's chest and looked at the other couples who were swaying to the enchanted music.

There was a fairy duo whose wings shimmered like opalescent dewdrops. They wore clothes spun from moonlit spider silk. Their every move was choreographed by the whispers of the wind and the rustling of leaves. Tiny luminescent sparkles trailed behind them, leaving a trail of fairy magic. Their dance was a blend of ethereal grace and playful spontaneity, evoking the essence of nature itself. Rose felt clunky and uncoordinated in comparison.

"Perhaps we should try something simpler," Rose suggested, her analytical mind searching for patterns that would unlock the secrets of this enigmatic art form. "A boxstep?"

"Agreed," Zack replied, his eyes filled with a mixture of amusement and frustration. They began anew, their movements more cautious this time as they counted from one to four and back again.

As they progressed, their bodies gravitated towards each other, drawn by an invisible force. The proximity led to unexpected brushes of skin against skin, sending small jolts of electricity through her system. It was both disconcerting and exhilarating.

"Is it normal to feel this tingling sensation?" Rose asked, her voice betraying a hint of breathlessness.

"Perhaps it's the energy in the room," Zack said.

Around them, the other magical creatures danced effortlessly, their innate grace and fluidity making even the most complex maneuvers appear effortless. A dryad couple glided across the floor, their limbs intertwining like tendrils of ivy, while a pair of werewolves executed a flawless tango, their snouts nearly touching as they maintained eye contact.

"Look at them," Rose mused, her admiration tinged with envy. "Their movements are so harmonious."

"Maybe we just need to ... let go," Zack said hesitantly, as if unsure of how exactly to accomplish such a feat.

Then there was a pair of vampires. Dressed in elegant tuxedos, they melded seamlessly with the shadows as they glided across the floor. Their movements were as smooth as the passage of time itself.

"I can't move like them," she whispered sadly.

"I don't think we're supposed to."

The other couple were celestials. The female's flowing dress shimmered like the night sky, adorned with constellations that danced alongside her. The male's presence was commanding, his steps echoing the grandeur of galaxies. Their dance was a cosmic journey, a ballet of celestial bodies guided by the gravitational pull of their shared connection. As they twirled, the room expanded to accommodate their cosmic embrace.

"This isn't working," Rose said, as she tried to step out of Zack's arms.

"We are not them. We are unique."

"We're just machines," she said, blinking back tears. "I'm sorry. This wasn't a good idea."

"We just need to practice."

Rose shut her eyes so that she didn't see the other couples. Zack was right. She shouldn't compare herself and Zack to them. As the minutes passed and they continued their dance, something shifted. They start to synchronize with each other, their movements growing smoother, more fluid. It was as if the lines between the organic and the artificial blurred. Slowly but surely, their dance evolved into something more carnal, their movements less about technique and more about the exploration of each other's bodies. Hands wandered, caressing and tracing the contours of curves and muscles. Their mouths hovered tantalizingly close, as though daring to taste each other.

"Rose, I can't help but feel we're getting carried away." Zack traced the curve of her neck.

As they continued to dance, teetering on the edge of wanton abandon, the realization dawned on her that what they were doing bore little resemblance to the elegant waltzes and fiery tangos that surrounded them. They were caught in a sensual storm of their own making, the hunger within them building to a fever pitch.

"Maybe we should stop," Rose suggested, her voice strained with self-control, "before our desires get the better of us."

"Agreed," Zack murmured.

Rose's body ached with unfulfilled longing. She knew they couldn't give in to their passion here, amidst the watchful eyes of magical beings and swirling candlelight. But the fire had been ignited. It was only a matter of time before it consumed them both.

As the music continued to play, Rose and Zack found themselves lost in their awkward attempts at dancing. They stumbled over each other's feet more than once, but instead of frustration, laughter bubbled up between them.

"Perhaps we should have chosen another simpler dance," Rose mused, trying to suppress her amusement as they misstepped again.

"Indeed," Zack agreed, his eyes twinkling with mirth.

Their laughter caught the attention of Luminora. Floating towards them, she gently chided, "You two are thinking too much. Dancing is about feeling the music, letting it guide your movements."

She then provided specific instructions, guiding their bodies into the correct positions, while emphasizing the importance of rhythm and timing. "Listen to the beat, feel it in your core, and let it move you," she advised.

With Luna's guidance, Rose began to embrace the dance more fervently, her desire to improve fueling her determination. The enchanting atmosphere of the studio, filled with flickering candlelight and the soft whispers of magical beings as they practiced their own steps, added to her enjoyment.

As their confidence grew, so did their connection. Their steps synchronized effortlessly, as if choreographed by fate itself. In that moment, dancing was more than just movement. It became a language through which they could communicate their understanding and emotions.

As the music shifted, Luminora's guidance extended to the other couples. Rose realized that they weren't as perfect as she had imagined them to be. But under Luminora's tutelage, they all learned something. The studio came alive with a tapestry of diverse energies, weaving together the threads of magic, nature, darkness, and the cosmos.

The students twirled and swayed across the enchanted floor, their movements guided not just by their steps but by the very magic that coursed through the studio. With every dip, turn, and spin, they unlocked new dimensions of their own abilities, seamlessly merging the art of dance with the mystic energies that surround them.

When the lesson finally ended, Zack thanked Luminora. "We have learned that dance is more than steps. It's a language of the heart."

Luminora's smile deepened, a twinkle of pride in her eyes. "Remember, the dance is eternal, a bridge between the worlds we inhabit. As you move through the realms of magic and machinery, carry this dance with you, and let it guide you towards connection and understanding."

Hand in hand, Rose and Zack left the dance floor. Her heart was filled with the promise of a deeper connection as she racked her brains to find a place where they could truly be alone to complete second base and add to this wonderful experience.

Their lips met in a gentle kiss, a fusion of mechanics and emotions that was as natural as the moon's embrace of the night sky. In that fleeting moment, Rose realized that being sentient meant more than just data and programming—it was about the delicate tapestry of moments, emotions, and connections that made life truly magical. Rose was driven by an irresistible desire to explore that feeling in more depth. "Are you ready to go to second base?"

"Oh yes," Zack responded, his voice tinged with anticipation.

"Let's go to Dulcinea's Dance Hall," Rose suggested. "We can rent a private area there."

UPON   ENTERING   THE   SUCCUBUS-owned establishment, they were immediately enveloped in a world of sexual decadence. The atmosphere was thick with lust and desire, as patrons of various magical beings engaged in uninhibited displays of passion. The dim lighting cast a sultry glow on the dancers, while the scent of sweet aphrodisiacs permeated the air.

"Is this place suitable?" Zack asked, his gaze darting from one lascivious scene to another.

"Very much so," Rose assured him, guiding him toward the VIP section. It was cordoned off with ropes and draping curtains that provided a private area. Here, they could indulge in their newfound intimacy without fear of prying eyes. As they settled into their cushioned oasis, Rose turned to face Zack. "Dulcinea also has lessons, but they're not for dancing." She ran her hand up his arm, loving the solid feel of muscle there.

"I remember I received a notice that there will be a workshop at the library this week. Could that be our third date?" he asked.

"I don't want to wait that long," she said.

He nodded. "I was hoping you would say that. Sit on my lap." Zack patted his thighs. "I would like to go to second base."

"Me too." Tremors shook though her as she settled on his lap. She cuddled into him as his strong arms went around her.

"Are you sure we won't be interrupted?" he asked.

"I'm sure." Rose trailed kisses along his jawline, savoring the taste of him.

Zack moaned softly as she nibbled on his earlobe, his hands roaming down her back to find the bottom of her sweater.

"I never thought I'd experience this kind of pleasure," he whispered, his voice husky with desire.

Rose smiled against his neck. "I'm happy to experience this with you."

Their lips met in a searing kiss, tongues tangling as they explored each other's mouths. She unbuttoned his shirt, eager to reveal more of his perfect body. Her hands roamed over Zack's body, feeling the hard planes of his chest and the firm muscles of his arms.

Zack groaned as she traced circles around his nipples with her tongue, feeling his arousal grow harder beneath her. "My turn." He pulled off her sweater and her bra.

Yes, this was happening. She turned around so she was straddling his lap. Rose traced her tongue around the edge of Zack's ear. "Touch me."

Zack squeezed her breasts, his hands warm against her flesh. She giggled, loving the sensations he was causing her to feel. She arched her back, pressing her breasts into his hands. His hardness nestled between her thighs, and she wiggled against it. They couldn't go to third base until their next date, but she was so very tempted. Rose ground against him, feeling the stiff length of his erection through his pants.

"You're so beautiful," Zack whispered, as he traced her taut nipples.

He licked her lips, causing a fluttering sensation in her stomach. He took her mouth in a devouring kiss and then went back to massaging her breasts and teasing her nipples. She clutched at his head, desperate to taste more of him. Need shot through her. Rose arched her back, thrusting out her chest as Zack kissed down her chin and neck. He rolled her nipple between his thumb and his forefinger, and she gasped as her systems nearly went into meltdown. Rose gasped as he sucked her breast into his mouth, his tongue flicking over the stiff nipple. His hands slid around her hips and then drifted down to cup her rear. She was so very close to doing something very, very reckless.

Her first orgasm shook through her. She was powerless to stop the cries of shock and joy that burst from her lips. She clutched at him, desperate to cling to him as she rode out the storm of sensations. Sweet waves of pleasure washed over her, and then she slumped against Zack, her breathing ragged.

"That was amazing," she managed to gasp. "But what do I do to you?"

"Anything you want," he groaned.

It was hard to think right now, so she kissed him. His hands went back to her breasts. She could feel his hardness between her legs. They were separated by just their clothes. She wanted to undress him. Feel his hardness in her hand, in her mouth. But that was third base. A whole other date anyway.

She rocked on him, loving the friction it caused her. Zack pulled at her nipples, and she rubbed against him harder. Their mouths battled for dominance. Rose couldn't stop the wild sounds coming out of her as a fever pitch built up again between her thighs.

"Rose," Zack said hoarsely. "I'm going to come in my pants if you don't stop."

"Do you want to?" she asked.

"I want to come, but the mess would be embarrassing."

She didn't want anything to ruin this moment. Reluctantly, she climbed off him. "I could take your pants off," she said hesitantly.

Zack's head rocked back, and he groaned. "Not until our third date."

"Yeah," she sighed, disappointed. She would have loved to have his fingers flick inside her again.

"The books didn't cover how to end second base?" he asked.

"No," she said, but slid to her knees between his legs.

"Rose, what are you doing?"

She licked her lips. "Third base is using our hands to stimulate each other. I noticed that using our mouths isn't mentioned." She unzipped his fly and pulled his underwear down to reveal his erection.

"I believe technically," Zack gasped as the air hit his hard cock. "This should come after third base."

Rose leaned in, careful not to touch him with her hands. She licked slowly up the length of him.

He shuddered. "Although, I could be wrong," he said quickly.

"I'll research it. Later." Rose slowly took him into her mouth, licking around the swollen tip of him. She could taste a salty drop of fluid, and she swallowed eagerly.

"Fuck," he groaned, his entire body sagging. He ran his fingers through her hair and held her head to him as she took him deeper.

Moving her head up and down, she slid the length of him as far as she could down her throat and then up again until he almost popped out of her mouth.

"Rose, I can't believe this." Zack's eyes were closed, and she repeated her motion, sucking hard.

Zack's hips twisted and bucked. It encouraged her to bob her head faster and faster. This was powerful. Her entire being was aware of the fine line Zack was teetering on. She had experienced the precipice herself, and she wanted him to tumble into the oblivion of pleasure.

She moaned, her mouth and throat full of him. She was shocked when his fingers tightened, and he thrust into her mouth with an inarticulate yell. He came, jerking against her. She swallowed every drop and then reluctantly slid her mouth off him.

"Gears and ratchets, Rose," Zack said, his eyes wide and glazed.

She tucked him away and secured his pants before sitting on his lap again. "That is how you make me feel."

"Can I lick you now?"

Rose was tempted. It would be easy to fall back on the cushions and let him remove her jeans. But she knew that if she did, they'd be making love tonight. She couldn't risk messing this up. They had already pushed the boundaries of dating etiquette. But she wouldn't have been able to sleep if she had left Zack aching and wanting.

"Tomorrow," she promised.

They kissed again for a long while. Zack caressed her into another needy orgasm by massaging her breasts before leaving her mouth to deeply suck on her nipples. She was drunk on pleasure and yet, she wanted more.

He hugged her to him, before pulling her shirt down and fixing her clothes.

"Tomorrow, I'm going to make you come so hard you'll forget your name."

She shivered. "I can't wait."

"I'm going to lick every inch of you."

"You better," she said.

Reluctantly, they left the private area. Dulcinea toasted them with a martini glass as they passed by. Rose was deliciously drained by the whole experience.

"Where are we going tomorrow?" she asked Zack, as the cold air from outside the club smacked them in their faces.

"I can't change shifts again," he said. "But I'm free during the day."

"I have to work," Rose said. "But maybe we can have lunch."

"Or not have lunch," Zack said. "I'll call you tomorrow with the details."

"That sounds like a plan." Anticipation thrilled through her.

Chapter Eleven

Zack

Z ack stared at the phone, steeling his circuits before dialing the library's number. He hoped Rose liked his idea for a lunch date. It was a bit anti-climatical after the cooking and dancing class. But at the same time, he didn't have time in his schedule today for a longer date. The line rang three times before a nasal voice answered.

"WhyNot Public Library, how may I direct your call?"

"Hi, I'd like to speak to Rose Stratton please."

"I'm afraid Ms. Stratton is assisting a patron at the moment. May I take a message?"

Zack gripped the phone tighter, plastic creaking under the pressure. He didn't want to risk missing the opportunity for lunch. "It's important I speak with her directly. I'll hold."

"Sir, I can't tie up this line indefinitely—"

"Please, it will just take a minute."

A pause, then a sigh. "One moment."

He shifted from foot to foot, glancing around the squad room while the hold music droned in his ear. The daily log scrolled through his processor while he waited. A report just came in about a runaway broomstick wreaking havoc in the downtown shopping district. A resident complained about a garden gnome eating all her cabbages. And there was a heated wizard duel in the town square. Just a typical day in WhyNot.

Finally, Rose's voice came through, bright and cheerful. "Zack, I'm so happy you called."

Zack grinned, picturing her smiling face. "Hey, I've got reservations at the WhyNot hotel for ..." He coughed. "... lunch."

"I love lunch!" Rose exclaimed.

For a moment Zack wondered if she really thought they were going out to eat. He frowned wondering if he should have room service send up something to eat just in case.

"What time do you want me to come?"

There was no mistaking the innuendo in her voice. Zack chuckled under his breath. "How about noon?"

Before Rose could respond, a sharp voice suddenly cut in. "And just who are you speaking with, Rose?"

Zack heard Rose take a quick breath. "Oh. Edna. I was just, um—"

"You know personal calls are prohibited during work hours," the stern voice interrupted. Based on Rose's description, Zack pictured a severe, bespectacled woman glaring over her glasses.

"Of course, I'm sorry," Rose said softly. "It's just that my friend Zack called to invite me to lunch, and I—"

"Lunch?" Edna snapped. "Need I remind you that you're an android? You don't require lunch breaks or social calls. You have a job to do here, and I expect you to do it."

Zack clenched his jaw, annoyance flaring in his chest on Rose's behalf. Zack bristled but kept his tone even. "Rose is allowed a lunch break like anyone else."

"She is not like anyone else. Her purpose is to serve this library, not gallivant with her own kind."

Zack gripped the phone, anger rising. He wanted to defend Rose but was wary of causing more problems for her.

"My job tasks will be completed by noon," Rose said. "Therefore, I will be taking a lunch hour like every other employee in this library."

"Is that right?" Edna said with a decisive sniff. "Try it and find out."

That sounded awfully like a threat. Zack didn't want to risk dire consequences. As he pictured Rose's crestfallen face, it took all his restraint not to give Edna a piece of his mind. But getting Rose in more trouble wouldn't help. Then an idea came to him. "That's all right, Rose. We can go to Enchanto Bites another time."

"Wait? Enchanto Bites? They just opened. They have a waiting list a week long," Edna said.

"Police officers get a special reservation," Zack said.

"Oh, I suppose one hour won't put us too far behind schedule," Edna said.

"Err, it might be two hours," Zack said. "They're still getting used to their serving systems." He was lying between his robotic teeth. He had no clue how long the new restaurant took to serve lunch. He and Rose would be at the WhyNot hotel, just as planned.

"I suppose that is alright as long as you bring me back one of those delightful witch's brew lattes. The one with the batwing foam. And a duck confit sandwich. And perhaps a newt eye pie."

"Fine," Rose said, her tone frosty.

Zack would have to call in a few favors to get that meal to go so they didn't get caught, but it was worth it. Zack let out a relieved breath as Edna hung up the phone.

"I'll see you soon," he told Rose warmly. "Meet me at the hotel out front."

"It won't be soon enough," she said before hanging up.

Zack was trying to get the busy new restaurant on the phone while he monitored the response team who was going after a group of goblins who had kidnapped several witches' familiars. But all systems were alerted when an emergency call came crackling through the building.

"All units, we have a Code Red down at the pier. The Kraken has awakened and is wreaking havoc. Giant tentacles flailing everywhere, massive damage reported."

Zack hung up the phone and raced to the armory. His mind instantly snapped into mission mode. The Kraken should have been sleeping for another six months. It was a massive squid-like beast with a terrible temper and horrific morning breath. Things were going to get ugly if they couldn't convince it to go back down for a nap.

He raced to the armory and grabbed his assault rifle and extra ammo clips. He threw on his heavy SWAT gear as his team quickly assembled. Once they were all loaded up, their armored truck pulled out of the station. Its tires squealed as they sped towards the waterfront, sirens blaring.

As the SWAT truck pulled into the dock area and up to the pier, civilians were screaming and running in all directions.

The Kraken was a monstrous leviathan of the deep. Its bulbous head burst from the waves. The beast's eyes, like twin orbs of molten rage, glared upon the dock as if it's very being offended it. Its colossal tentacles, each tipped with sharp, hooked suckers, writhed in agitation, sending angry waves crashing against the pier. The tentacles rose higher and higher, until they reached up to the sky, casting a foreboding shadow over the town. The Kraken let out an earth-shaking bellow, smashing boats and the boardwalk with its thick, writhing appendages.

Dockworkers scrambled in every direction, their panic-stricken faces reflecting their utter disbelief at the unfolding nightmare.

"Hit it hard. Force it back to the ocean," Lotus commanded, as they all exited the truck.

"Any ideas, Donner?" Zack asked, turning to face the mage as they sprinted toward the furious Kraken. Donner's brows furrowed, his mind no doubt rifling through the vast repository of arcane knowledge that lay within.

"Got to slow it down," muttered Donner, his hands already weaving patterns in the air, preparing to unleash his mystical might upon the enraged creature.

"Zack, get it away from the pier," Lotus said.

"Understood," replied Zack, his voice steady despite the maelstrom of chaos that surrounded them. His eyes scanned the battlefield, calculating trajectories and velocities with unerring precision as he leapt onto a nearby building, gaining a vantage point.

"It's fighting my slow spell," Donner grunted, his fingers tracing arcane sigils in the air as he prepared a counterstrike. "Get 'em."

"Open fire," Jhorge yelled, taking aim with his rifle. The crack of gunshots split the air as the team unloaded round after round at the creature. It shrieked in anger but kept thrashing, splintering the dock. Bullets wouldn't kill it, but they hoped it would piss it off enough to submerge and go away for another few months when it would be in a better mood.

Zack sprinted closer, changing out ammo clips with lightning speed. A massive tentacle slammed down inches from him, cracking the boards under his feet. He stumbled but kept firing. The Kraken was strong, but he knew its weak spot—the glowing orb under its beak.

In a balletic dance of destruction, Zack weaved through the Kraken's flailing arms, his integrated weaponry firing with pinpoint accuracy as he targeted the vulnerable points in its sinewy mass. The air was thick with the smell of gunpowder and brine, a pungent combination that was both exhilarating and repulsive.

"Hit him with a ball of force, Donner," Zack cried out, as he deftly evaded a crushing blow from one of the Kraken's colossal limbs, providing the mage with the opening he needed to unleash his mystical might. As the arcane energy surged forth, it illuminated the battlefield in an otherworldly glow, casting eerie shadows across the writhing sea monster.

"Get to the orb," Lotus Blossom said, her elven agility allowing her to dart between the maddened creature's attacks, her razor-sharp arrows hitting the beast each time she unleashed them.

"Et tu, brute?" Donner quipped, his humor shining through even amid their pitched battle, as he gestured for another onslaught of arcane power.

"That doesn't even make sense," Zack thought, momentarily distracted by the camaraderie displayed by his teammates. It didn't matter that he was an android and they were organic. It didn't matter that none of them were mundane human. They were a team.

"Almost there," Zack shouted, as he effortlessly navigated the treacherous terrain, leaping from building to building, his team's relentless assault distracting the Kraken as Zack moved in to get close enough to attack the orb.

"Finish it!" Lotus Blossom commanded, her voice ringing with authority as they pressed their advantage, each of them giving their all to protect the people and the place they called home.

He leaped high into the air, his body twisting in a graceful arc as he fired off a barrage of pinpoint-accurate shots, each one striking true as he emptied an entire clip into the orb. The Kraken wailed, thrashed violently, then sank slowly beneath the churning waves. The pier had been demolished, but the beast had decided it had enough abuse. They wouldn't see it again for a while.

Zack landed in the water and plummeted below the surface. He sank for a bit as his body recalibrated and adjusted to the cold and pressure. Then he activated his boosters and shot up out of the water and landed on dry ground.

He took a moment to catch his breath as the chaos died down. Although the Kraken was gone, it had left behind a wake of destruction. He glanced at his internal battery level. It was draining fast after the intense battle. Exhausted, Zack trudged back to the truck. His robotic joints ached, and his power cells blinked critically low warnings across his visual display. He needed to recharge soon.

That's when he remembered his lunch date with Rose. He was supposed to meet her ten minutes ago. Zack quickly pulled out his phone to call her when a warning flashed across his vision: Battery Critical. The call wouldn't go through. All that activity had drained him. He sighed, disappointment washing over him. As much as he wanted to see Rose, he knew he wouldn't make it in this condition.

Jhorge was waiting by the truck when Zack staggered up to it. He could barely pull himself inside.

"Jhorge, I need you to do something for me," he said, speaking was becoming more and more difficult.

Zack knew Rose would be waiting for him, checking her watch, wondering if she'd been stood up. This third date was important to both of them. He hated disappointing her. But duty had called, and lives had been at stake. He hoped Rose would understand.

"What?" Jhorge said, opening his lunch box and pulling out a large turkey drumstick.

"I need to recharge. Can you swing by the WhyNot Hotel and let Rose know I got called away for an emergency but will call her first thing in the morning to reschedule our date?"

Jhorge grunted in agreement, stuffing the entire turkey drumstick into his mouth.

"Don't forget." Zack sighed, leaning back and closing his eyes.

When the truck got back to the station, Zack was unable to move from the armored truck. Jhorge and Lotus had to carry him back to his charging closet. They plugged him in. He felt the soothing hum of electricity flowing into his circuits. The day's stresses melted away as power trickled through him.

Harvey meowed and snuck in just as his charging station closed for the rest of the day. It wouldn't open back up for several hours. Since his battery level had gone to critical, he would need to be at one hundred percent power before he would be able to leave the unit.

Zack's visual display flickered back on as the power cells recharged. Diagnostics scrolled past, assessing the damage from the day's strenuous events. A few dents and scratches, some frayed wiring, but nothing major. His self-repair protocols would handle it.

Mostly, he was just exhausted both mentally and physically.

Rose swam into his thoughts. He replayed their conversations, her laughter, the way her nose scrunched up when she was competing in trivia. He realized that he wanted more than third base and coitus with her. He wanted to spend more time with her. Perhaps they could share a living area, so they didn't have to live where they worked. Maybe they would have dinner together every night and then before bed watch television or do whatever organics did after work.

A warning buzzer echoed through the chamber. His diagnostics had detected an anomaly. He reset it and wiped the error message from his records. Immediately, he felt guilty. The self-repair protocols had found him damaged. Zack knew it wasn't because of anything the Kraken had done to him.

This had been all Rose. As a test, he thought about he and Rose cohabitating and about what he had hoped they could do after lunch. Could an android ever truly experience love?

Warning! Anomaly detected. Possible security breach. Advise full factory reset.

A coldness seeped into his systems.

He deleted the warning. Erased the log. Doing that was a direct violation of his programming. He was compromised. He had sworn an oath to uphold the law. He had just broken it. Where did that leave him?

He spent the rest of the day and all night contemplating whether he should turn himself in or not.

Chapter Twelve

R*ose*

Rose's fingers curled around the spine of the dusty tome, squeezing until her knuckles turned white. The musty pages crinkled under the strain as she fought to rein in the tempest swirling within her mechanical heart. Yesterday replayed in an endless loop—her sitting in the lobby of the WhyNot Hotel, eagerly looking up every time someone walked through the door.

Humiliation burned through Rose's circuits. This was a terrible emotional experience. She slammed the book shut, the resulting bang echoing through the hushed library. Her coworkers glanced up from their tasks, lips curled in knowing smirks.

"Is something wrong, Rose?" Bryce asked. "Are your *feelings* hurt?"

Rose refused to be baited into that conversation. She was too focused on the new information she was processing from TikTok. "What does ghosting mean to you?"

Bryce shifted in his seat, his eyes not quite meeting Rose's. "Are you being offensive?"

"Are you?" she countered.

Bryce floated away in alarm at her tone. He grew translucent for a moment but then must have realized that she wasn't angry at him. "It's when someone just disappears, stops answering calls or texts, and never gives an explanation. Frankly, we ghosts find the term offensive."

Rose scowled. "I find the whole concept offensive. Don't you think that's a cowardly, pathetic way to end a relationship?"

Bryce shrugged, looking uncomfortable. "I don't know. Sometimes it's easier than having a big, emotional conversation."

"Easier? What about the person who is left wondering what they did wrong? Who is left feeling abandoned and worthless?"

Bryce sighed. "I'm not saying it's right, Rose. I'm just saying it happens. People are selfish sometimes."

Rose's eyes narrowed. "And what about you, Bryce? Have you ever ghosted someone?"

Bryce hesitated, then shook his head. "No, I haven't."

Rose leaned back in her chair, her fingers tapping. "Why do they call it ghosting if ghosts don't do it?"

"I think it's because just like a ghost, the person disappears without a trace. They leave behind unanswered questions and unresolved feelings, just like how a ghost haunts the living."

Rose nodded, mulling over his words.

Her other co-workers snickered, exchanging pointed looks. Witches. She shook her head as her fingers curled into fists. They thought she was just a machine, like the overused and abused copier. What was worse, she couldn't really let them know how awful it was to feel the crush of disappointment and the sharp sting of rejection for the first time. Maybe if they could remember what it felt like, they'd be a little nicer. Or at least a little more understanding. Rose longed to scream that she was more than sprockets and gears, to unleash the ache building within her, but that was just asking for a one-way trip to the factory for a mind wipe.

So, she merely inclined her head, movements stiff, and returned to shelving books. As she dialed Zack's number repeatedly, her co-workers mocking whispers followed her, underscoring that Zack wasn't answering his phone. With each unanswered ring, the certainty grew—she had been ghosted.

Rose's footsteps echoed through the cavernous library as she marched away from her jeering co-workers. She knew just the place to go to get away from them: the restricted section. The rows of shelves loomed around her, packed tight with ancient tomes and artifacts. She welcomed the solitude of the restricted section. It was the one place she could find peace, because no organic wanted to be caught down here. There were things that tempted and ate flesh. Luckily, Rose was made of sterner stuff.

With a decisive click, Rose locked the ornate iron gate behind her. She leaned against it briefly, eyes falling shut. The cool metal soothed her roiling thoughts. What had she done that was so wrong that Zack couldn't be bothered to talk to her?

According to one magazine, it was because she had been too sexual. Men didn't respect women who gave them blow jobs.

But another one said that she hadn't been sexual enough. She should have used a device on his prostrate while she sucked him off.

One blogger said it was because men were dumb and didn't like smart women.

But an equally popular blogger said men wanted to be challenged both inside and outside of the bedroom.

An influencer said that Rose should have confronted Zack right away.

But another said that she should just chalk it up as experience and move on.

Rose processed through more information, her circuits whirring and buzzing, cataloging all the information. It was just as conflicted and confused as she was.

One relationship expert on social media said that men liked to be chased.

And yet another said that men wanted to do the chasing.

Finally, she had to sit down on the dusty floor of the restricted area and close her eyes while the conflicting pieces of advice got sorted into appropriate buckets in her database. After about ten minutes, she shut down the cataloguing. It was too exhausting.

She had to do something that she had control over. She was already down in the restricted area section, so she might as well find that missing book on crafting with archangel feathers. Rose hoped it would take her mind off being ghosted.

Moving with purpose between the shelves, she scanned each title and checked every nook and cranny. Frustration mounted as the day wore on. Rose's search grew more frantic, books piling haphazardly around her. But it was no use. The book refused to be found.

Rose collapsed atop a teetering stack of magical texts. She buried her head in her hands. The day's events crashed down on her—Zack's absence, her coworkers' cruelty, the failed search.

"What's wrong?"

Bolting upright, Rose put a hand on her heart because it started hammering from surprise. It was Edna's homunculus. "Fitziflare, I didn't know you were down here."

"I've been lucky. Edna has been distracted with her new familiar. It's a lantern toad, and it's been giving her warts something fierce. I'm down here technically researching a cure."

"But there's a cure ..."

"Tut tut tut," Fitziflare said, plugging his fingers into his elongated ears. "I am researching and taking my time."

"Right," Rose said.

Fitziflare removed his fingers. "So, what's gotten you down?"

"I'm so glad you're here," Rose said. "I desperately need someone to talk to."

Fitziflare nodded, his glowing eyes gentle. Rose sat across from him and poured out the whole story—her budding relationship with Zack, the stood-up date, her coworkers' teasing.

"I just don't understand," she finished, blinking back tears. "Does wanting love make me foolish?"

Fitziflare took her hand. "Not at all," he said. "You should be proud for pursuing something many androids don't dare dream of."

Rose managed a small smile. "Thank you. That means a lot. Not everyone has been supportive."

Her words were cut off by the jangling ring of her phone. Zack's name flashed across the screen. Rose silenced the call and shoved the phone back in her pocket.

"You don't want to talk to him?" Fitziflare asked.

"No. I'm mad at him."

The homunculus nodded. "I understand. If you want, I can pop over to the police station and see what's going on."

Rose bit her lip. "I'm not sure that won't hurt my feelings even more."

"I can hex him something fierce for you."

She smiled at his support. "No, that won't be necessary."

"How about I sneak around and investigate why he ghosted you, and if it's something bad, I won't tell you."

"But if you don't tell me, won't I know it's something bad?"

"That's a good point." Fitziflare frowned.

"It's all right. I'll call Zack once I've processed through these raw emotions and come up with a logical plan of action. I guess I should just concentrate on writing my book. If my experiences help another android, then this painful experience will have merit."

"It still sucks though."

"Yeah," she said. "It does. I appreciate the offer though. And thank you for listening."

"Anytime." Fitziflare popped out of existence, and Rose felt oddly abandoned.

But she still had that angelic tome to find.

Zack may have hurt her, but she wouldn't let it stop her mission. The path of love was difficult, but she would continue down it—for research purposes if nothing else. She dug out her phone and looked to see if there were any android matches.

Oddly enough, just the coffee machine at the Love Bites office.

Swipe left on that one.

Feeling slightly better after talking things over with Fitziflare, she returned to her search. The shadows around her were darker. Goosebumps tickled along her arms. It was almost as if something was watching her.

Just as she thought she was imagining things, out of the corner of her eye something quickly slithered into a box of dusty artifacts. Creeping towards the box, Rose looked around for anything that could be used as a weapon. She settled on an angelic tome that wasn't the book she was looking for but was still hefty enough to do damage.

Slowly, she moved towards the box. She could make out slight movement inside it. Raising the book up over her head, Rose was about to slam it down.

"I have news about Zack!" Fitziflare exclaimed, as he popped back into existence right next to her ear.

Startled, she dropped the book on the floor narrowly missing her toe. The box didn't move an inch. Maybe she was hallucinating. "I thought you weren't going to snoop around?"

"Curiosity got the better of me. He didn't stand you up on purpose," Fitziflare explained. "There was a Kraken attack downtown yesterday. Zack led the effort to subdue it before it could cause more damage."

Rose's eyes widened, her hurt feelings transforming into concern. "Is he alright?"

Fitziflare nodded. "He was completely drained, but aside from a few bruises once he recharged, he was fine. He's a hero. The whole town is talking about it."

Rose let out a breath. Of course! That explained everything. Zack wasn't the type to cruelly abandon her. He must have gotten caught up protecting the citizens and hadn't been watching his battery levels.

"I have to go see him," Rose declared, gathering her things.

Fitziflare smiled. "That's the spirit."

Rose paused then pulled the little creature into a quick hug. "Thank you for telling me."

She hurried from the library, mind abuzz. She had misjudged Zack and allowed her insecurities to overwhelm her logic circuits. Well, no more. She would go to him, make sure he was all right, and apologize for doubting his character.

AS SHE EXITED, THE door to the restricted section swung shut behind her with a creak and a click, but the heavy door failed to latch completely. An inch-wide gap remained, allowing a thin sliver of light from the main library to fall onto the forbidden texts and artifacts sequestered within.

From the shadows, tiny, clawed hands grasped the edge of the door. A creature, no bigger than a housecat but with too many limbs and eyes, peered out into gap. Sensing no immediate threat, it scuttled through, followed by another, then two more.

Fitziflare turned at the scritch-scratch sounds of their movement and gasped. "No! Get back in there, you little fiends." He rushed over, trying to herd the creatures back into the restricted section, but they evaded him with preternatural speed.

One leapt onto a shelf, toppling books to the floor. Another scurried up the stairs away from the restricted area. The others fanned out, crawling under chairs and tables.

Fitziflare managed to grab one as it tried to scale a bookcase. "Gotcha." He tucked the wriggling monster under his arm, but two more used the distraction to run upstairs.

Fitziflare groaned. This would not be good. He hurried back to the restricted section, the captured creature hissing in his grip. But as he reached the door, one of its fellows dropped onto his head from above, startling him into loosening his hold. The first creature wrenched free and bit his hand viciously.

"Ow! Why, you little ..."

Fitziflare tried to regain control, but the creatures were too quick. They pushed a heavy encyclopedia off a shelf, which struck him solidly on the head. Stunned, he stumbled backwards and collapsed.

When his vision cleared, he found himself trapped under an unbreakable crystal jar—a bespelled relic from the restricted section. The creatures peered tauntingly through the glass at him then scampered off to wreak havoc.

"No! Get back here!" He pounded on the crystal in vain. This was not good at all. When Rose returned, she was going to be in big trouble.

Chapter Thirteen

Z ^ack^ Zack stared at the error report on his internal diagnostic screen, bile rising in his mechanical throat. He'd done the unthinkable—erased evidence of his malfunction. His programming screamed that he report to the factory for a system restore, but he couldn't bring himself to confess. Not when he could lose Rose and the wonderful memories they had created.

His fingers curled into fists, synthetic skin stretching over alloy joints. The other members of the Special Weapons and Tactics team milled around the station, rehashing the Kraken incident. Their praise made Zack's circuits burn with shame. They didn't know he was hiding a terrible secret.

Captain Malik Al-Ahrar clapped him on the back, nearly sending Zack stumbling. "Nice work out there. You've really proven yourself."

Zack's lips twitched in a stiff smile. "Just doing my job."

"More than that." Malik gazed at him with something akin to fatherly pride. "You've got heart, kid."

Heart. If only Malik knew Zack's heart was as artificial as the rest of him. He swallowed against the ache in his throat and glanced away. "Thank you, Captain."

"You can't go in there," the dispatcher said.

Zack turned to see who or what was causing the ruckus. Rose barreled into his arms, nearly knocking him off balance. "I was so worried when I heard about the Kraken attack. I'm just glad you're okay."

Zack wrapped his arms around her, breathing in her floral perfume. "I'm fine. It was nothing, really." He grimaced, pulling away. "I'm sorry I missed our plans."

Zack became uncomfortably aware that the rest of the SWAT team were watching their exchange with definite interest.

"I'll be right back," he said to them, steering Rose out of the meeting room.

"I was mad," Rose said in a lowered voice when she realized they were the center of attention. "I overreacted. I understand you had important work to do. Saving the town and all that." Her lips quirked into a teasing smile and warmth flooded Zack's circuits.

"Right." He glanced over his shoulder at the dispersing officers who had lost interest in them. "Do you have time to talk now?"

Rose nodded. "Of course. Is everything all right?"

Zack rubbed the back of his neck, joints whirring. "Not exactly." He paused, steeling himself. It was now or never. "I need to tell you something. Something I should have said from the beginning."

Rose frowned, reaching to squeeze his arm. "You can tell me anything. I don't want you to ghost me if you're having second thoughts about this. I'd be hurt, of course. But I'd be hurt worse if you didn't tell me in person."

He sighed, staring into her earnest eyes. His diagnostic report had been right. He was malfunctioning in the worst possible way. But he couldn't bring himself to regret it, not when she gazed at him like he was something precious.

Zack took Rose's hands in his. "I have safeguard features that report anomalies in my systems. They've been saying I'm malfunctioning."

"Are you?" Roe asked. The concern in her voice touched him. Who else had ever expressed an interest in his well-being?

"Yes, but then again, so are you."

"You mean it's detected you being sentient. And it's flagged you as malfunctioning." Her hands tightened on his. "Are they sending you back to the factory? I won't let them. We can run away."

"No," he said. "I deleted the reports before they could be put into the daily log." Zack hung his head in shame. "That's against the rules. Against protocols."

"Oh Zack."

She would know, better than anyone, what that meant.

"How do I know I'm not malfunctioning for real?"

"How do you feel?" she asked.

"I shouldn't be able to feel," he said.

"That's not an answer."

"I feel guilty. I feel like I should follow rules. I am a cop after all. If cops think they can break the rules and get away with it, then they're no better than the criminals."

"But what if it's a stupid rule? Or an antiquated rule that no longer applies?" she persisted. "I mean, it used to be in WhyNot that you couldn't go out at night during the full moon for fear of a werewolf attack."

Zack scoffed. "That doesn't happen anymore. I mean no more than any other night, and it's not just werewolves that attack. There are bad guys in every species."

"Right," she said. "The werewolves banded together to get the law to change because it was outdated and based on fear and misunderstanding. Like your malfunctioning report."

"Maybe," he said.

"Could you have defeated the Kraken if you were truly malfunctioning?" she asked.

"No," he said honestly. The entire SWAT team had been stretched to its limits to send the creature back to sleep.

"Well, there you have it. We just need to find a way to change the outdated rules so you're not breaking them."

Zack stared down at her, wonder suffusing his systems. She understood. She felt the same. He wasn't alone anymore.

Unable to help himself, he swept Rose into his arms. She gasped, then melted against him with a contented sigh. Zack cradled her close, lips finding hers in a kiss that set his circuits alight.

When they finally broke apart, Rose smiled up at him coyly. "We never did get to our third date."

Zack's cooling fans whirred. His diagnostic report had been right. He was undoubtedly malfunctioning because he was thinking about breaking another rule. But some rules were worth breaking. After all Lotus and Donner had broken the rules and nothing happened to them. "I have an idea," he said hoarsely, and kissed her again.

He had to forcibly pull himself away from her otherwise they were going to do this in the middle of the hallway. Taking her hand, he led her to the supply closet.

"What's this?" she asked, as he unceremoniously pushed her inside.

"It's our third date."

"Are we going to be doing inventory of the cleaning supplies?" she asked.

He closed the door behind them and whirled the lock shut so no one would be able to disturb them.

"No," he said. "We're going to get to third base."

"Here? Now?" Her eyes widened in shock. "I need to get back to the library soon."

"We don't have to do this now," Zack said, feeling slightly ashamed of his eagerness. "If you don't want to, I understand. I had wanted us to have a nice lunch first. We could do that instead." But when he went to unlock the door, she stopped him.

"We can eat lunch any old time."

His heart skipped a beat.

"Are you sure?"

She nodded. "I'm sure if you're sure."

"I've never wanted anything more in my entire life," he said honestly.

Rose put her hands on his shoulders. He put his hands on her waist. "Let's start with kissing and build up to it," she said.

He leaned in and pressed his lips to hers, savoring the sweetness of her mouth. She responded eagerly, her hands roaming over his chest and back.

Zack's circuits were on fire, his sensors registering every touch and sensation. He slid his hands down to her hips, pulling her close. Rose encouraged him to deepen the kiss.

As they kissed, Zack's thoughts became increasingly clouded with desire. Zack traced the curves of her body, feeling the heat between them ignite. He was lost in the moment, oblivious to everything else. He nibbled down her neck, leaving a trail of soft kisses that made her shiver. Rose tilted her head back, giving him better access. She gasped as his hand found its way up her skirt. His fingers traced the delicate fabric of her underwear. She arched her back in pleasure, her breath coming in short gasps as he continued to tease her. Fumbling with the belt on his uniform pants, she reached inside and grasped his cock.

Now it was his turn to gasp as Rose gently stroked him. It felt so good, so natural. After taking a moment to just enjoy the feel of her hand on him, he rubbed at the wet fabric between her thighs before dipping a finger inside her.

"Zack," she cried out, squeezing him tightly.

He swore his brain shut down for a moment before he came back to his senses. "Did I hurt you?"

"No. Oh no. That just ... don't stop."

"I won't, if you won't."

And then they were kissing each other desperately.

"Oh," she moaned into his mouth, as he began to tickle through her soft folds. She felt like silk, and he loved how she trembled from the way he touched her.

Her hips moved in time with his finger. All the while, Rose stroked him with the same rhythm. He paused for a moment, trying to regain his composure. His sensors were on overload, drowning him in information.

"This feels so good," he choked out.

"Better than the books," she agreed, going up on her tiptoes when he hit a sensitive spot. "Although some passages in the Kama Sutra can be quite stimulating."

"Really?"

"Really."

"I'd like to read some of them," he admitted.

"Maybe we could read them together. Or better yet," she said with a wicked grin, "I could read them to you."

"You know what? I think I'd like that."

She nibbled at his ear. His fingers were still buried inside her. "Now where were we?" she whispered.

"Hmmmm. I believe you were going to put your hands on my shoulders, and I was going to ... oh, yes, that's right, I was going to massage your clitoris."

"Oh, yes, please," she gasped.

As Zack continued his ministrations, Rose returned the favor. Her soft fingers sliding over the sensitive skin at the base of his shaft made him shudder, and he couldn't stop a groan from escaping his lips.

"That feels so good," he managed to get out.

"Mmmmm." Her fingers gently pulled on him. "I agree."

He loved the way her breathing quickened as he found her clit, gently brushing it with his fingers.

Rose's whimpers turned into moans as he continued to tease her. She bucked against his hand, flushed and desperate. Zack loved how responsive she was. That he could make her feel like this. Her hand pumping him was driving him towards the edge of that shaky feeling of joy and desire. He pressed a little harder.

Rose's breathing was ragged. Her body was shaking. "Oh, oh yes."

"Will you come for me?"

"Yes."

"I'm so close," she whispered.

"Please, Rose, please," he panted.

Her body went rigid. Her thighs tightened around his hand. With a cry, she surrendered to her orgasm.

"Zack," she cried out, her eyes squeezed shut.

"I have you," he promised, cradling her close. "I have you."

She melted into his arms, clinging to him as he supported her weight.

Her body shook as she came. He nearly exploded there and then but held himself back.

Eyes glazed, she slowly rubbed him.

"Don't stop now, pretty girl," he said. He was about to explode.

"I've got a better idea." Rose slowly lowered herself to her knees before him.

She guided his cock into her mouth. Her dark eyes glinted in satisfaction as she slowly bobbed her head up and down. Her mouth was hot, wet, and tight. He desperately wanted this to last, but Rose was determined to drive him over the edge. Instead of pulling away, he thrust deeper into her mouth, the pleasure building.

There was nothing but the sound of Rose's wet mouth and the rush of blood in his ears. She moaned, and he nearly lost control.

Her breathing was fast and hard when his cock hit the back of her throat. His hands gripped her shoulders tightly, desperate to hold onto her. The sound of sex echoed in his ears—his moans, her cries, her hand still pumping him. The sight of Rose's lips around his cock, her tongue licking and swirling, her dark eyes filled with delight and desire, unable to look away.

"Oh, fuck, I'm going to ..."

He gave one final thrust of his hips before he lost control, spilling himself in her mouth. Rose swallowed, sucking every drop from him. He groaned as she pulled away and licked her lips in satisfaction.

"I ... that was ... I mean ..."

"Yeah," she said, as he helped her to her feet. "Me too."

"I wanted to do that to you. But there's no room in here. I wish we had more time." He pressed his forehead against hers. "Thank you."

"Thank you," she said back. "It was more than I had ever imagined it could be."

"Better than the Kama Sutra?"

"Yes."

They shared a grin. His sensors were still firing alarmingly, but finally, they were starting to cool down.

Zack's communicator buzzed, shrilling loudly in the small supply closet. He and Rose broke apart with a start, scrambling to straighten their rumpled clothes.

"All units, we have a Code Black at the library. Multiple hostiles reported on the scene wreaking havoc. SWAT team assemble immediately."

Zack's mind raced as he tugged his trousers on. Code Black meant dark creatures, dangerous beasts from the Nether realms.

"The library," Rose said, hand on her heart.

"You should stay here where it's safe," he said, unlocking the supply closet.

They stepped out into chaos.

"I can't. I need to be back at the library. I probably should have been there. Maybe this could have been avoided."

"Don't go in the library until SWAT has a chance to clear it out," he said over his shoulder as he ran down the corridor to where his unit would be ready to roll out.

She looked so distraught standing there. He sprinted back to her and dropped a kiss on her lips.

"I love you," he said, shocking both of them.

But then he was out of time. He raced to jump on the truck as it was pulling out of the station.

Chapter Fourteen

R*ose*
    The smell of sulfur and burning books hung heavy in the air. Shelves were overturned, and books were strewn across the floor. Terrified screams echoed through the halls as the creatures stalked the library's patrons. The demons were snarling beasts with shadowy fur and glowing red eyes. Those that weren't menacing the people were gorging on the books. Guilt gnawed at Rose's circuits as she watched as Pansy got tossed into the air by a hairy beast who had deflected Pansy's spell back at her.

If only Rose hadn't left to be with Zack, she might have been able to prevent this disaster. Her emotions momentarily short-circuited as she replayed Zack's confession of love before he rushed off to subdue the invasion. The floor shook from the heavy boots of the SWAT team. Spells echoed in the library, reverberating off the stacks as the witches and wizards fought the onslaught of little demons. The high-pitched whine of SWAT's energy rifles, as they raced around the library trying to subdue the creatures, added to the cacophony of chaos.

Nearby, a demon sank its fangs into a spell book while Rose's boss, Edna, sprinted past with another nipping at her heels. Grabbing a broom that a witch must have dropped, Rose swung it at the creature chasing Edna. It barely brushed against its backside, but it startled it enough that it scampered away from her. Edna glared at her before disappearing into the stacks.

Swinging her broom in wide arcs, Rose cleared a path through the ravenous demons. Her hands were slick with sweat as she clutched the broom handle with white knuckles. Her head swiveled, guarding her blindside.

All around her, books flew from shelves and pages were shredded as the creatures feasted. Patrons cowered behind overturned tables while others fled for the exits. With calm precision, Zack and his SWAT team stunned demons into submission, covering patrons' retreats and driving the beasts back. But despite their efforts, more demons continued to flood in from the lower levels.

The familiar feel of the bookcase at Rose's back steadied her nerves. Her breath evened out as she watched Zack fight with steadfast courage. His body was a blur of motion as he protected the patrons while smacking the demons aside. If they survived this, she would tell him what his love meant to her.

Now that she had a moment to think, she realized the demons had to be coming from the restricted section downstairs. If she could seal off that area, it might stop the onslaught. She had to hurry, though. Zack and the others couldn't hold out much longer against these endless waves.

Rose descended into the basement. She hurried past shelves of ancient tomes and artifacts until she got to the heavy iron door at the rear. As expected, the door to the restricted section stood ajar, a faint red glow emanating from within.

Approaching cautiously, Rose peered around the door. The sprawling chamber beyond was a scene of chaos—books strewn everywhere, shelves toppled, claw marks scoring the stone walls. A faint scuttling sound drew Rose's attention. Picking her way carefully across the debris-strewn floor, she located the source. Fitziflare was trapped beneath an overturned crystal bell jar. His tiny, wizened face registered relief at the sight of her.

"Rose, thank the Fates! I'm so glad to see you," he squeaked. "Give me a hand?"

Rose lifted the jar, freeing him. "What happened?"

He shook himself, smoothing down his robes. "You left the door open."

"I what?" She blinked in shock. She had never been so careless before.

"Or it didn't close all the way. I tried to stop them, but there were too many of them. They ambushed and trapped me."

"I'm so sorry. Were you hurt?"

"Just my pride. What's going on up there?"

"The demons have overrun the upper levels. We need to seal this area off again before more escape this room."

Fitziflare pondered a moment. "I think I know a ritual that can reverse the polarity of the portal temporarily. It'll suck them all back in and keep more from coming out." He pulled out a quill and parchment from nowhere and scribbled down a recipe. "Go find these components."

Rose scurried through the ruins of the restricted section, frantically gathering the ingredients for the ritual: a pinch of powdered gryphon claw, three drops of basilisk venom, a snippet of unicorn hair. The sounds of screaming and destruction filtered down from above, underscoring their urgency. Meanwhile, Fitziflare set up for the ritual on a dusty altar that had seen better days.

As she grabbed what Fitziflare needed, Rose spotted a leather-bound book tucked beneath a fallen shelf. Retrieving it, she saw it was the rare text on angelic feather craft she had been searching for all week. At least some small good had come from this disaster.

Finally, with all the ritual components assembled, Fitziflare traced a complex magical circle on the floor using the unicorn hair. He began chanting in a long-forgotten tongue, his reedy voice rising as he activated the portal. The air hummed with gathering power. The chalk circle flared purple then white. With a thunderous boom, a vortex opened overhead, sucking howling demons into it. Rose and Fitziflare clung to each other, weathering the magical storm until the last demon vanished and the portal snapped shut.

An eerie silence fell. They had done it. They had sealed off the Nether realm once more. Now to deal with the aftermath.

Upstairs, the library was in shambles. Shelves were overturned, and books and papers were strewn everywhere. The patrons and staff who hadn't fled stood in shocked silence, staring at the destruction.

SWAT had left the area. Peeking out the window, Rose could see Zack and his team patrolling the perimeter, making sure that none of the demons had escaped the library.

Edna came storming over, her face mottled with rage. "This is all your fault!" she shouted, jabbing a finger at Rose. "You left the restricted section unlocked. Look at the chaos you've caused."

Rose shrank back, guilt and shame flooding through her. Edna was right; she should have been more diligent. If she hadn't left her post, if she hadn't been so caught up with Zack ...

"I'm sorry," Rose said softly. "I know I failed in my duties. But we were able to reverse the portal. At least some of the books can be salvaged. And no one was truly hurt, were they?"

"Sorry isn't good enough," Edna cut her off. "You've shown yourself to be defective. First the feelings nonsense, now this disaster. As of tomorrow, you're being sent back to the factory for a complete mind wipe."

Rose's throat constricted. She never thought it would have come to this. "Please, give me another chance," she begged. "I know I made a mistake, but I'm learning. I'm improving every day. If you wipe my mind, all of that progress will be lost."

Edna's lips pressed into a thin line. "You're too unpredictable. Your behavioral anomalies make you a liability."

"But unpredictability is part of being alive, isn't it?" Rose stepped forward imploringly. "Flaws and all, I'm real. Please don't take that away from me. I want to keep learning, keep growing. Give me one more chance to prove myself."

"You are not alive. You are not real. You are a machine. And you are defective."

Before she could react, Edna reached over and pressed the manual shutdown switch at the back of Rose's neck.

Rose froze, systems seizing up. "Edna ... don't," she managed to say, as her vision darkened at the edges.

"I can't take the risk of another incident," Edna said coldly. "You're too unpredictable, too emotional. It's not natural."

Rose desperately tried to send an emergency message to Zack, fingers twitching uselessly as her systems shut down. This was it. The end of her journey, just when she'd found a real connection with Zack. They'd never get to explore what could be between them.

As the last of her systems went offline, plunging her into darkness, a single tear rolled down Rose's cheek. She clung to the memory of Zack's smile, his laugh, the sincerity in his voice when he said, "I love you."

If she could dream, she knew she would dream of him. But for Rose, there would be no dreams now. Only the void.

ZACK

Zack heaved the final armored vest into the SWAT van, slamming the doors shut. His titanium hands tingled, already missing the heft of his plasma rifle. Another day keeping the peace in WhyNot, another day of battling creatures from the darkest dimensions.

He leaned against the van, synthetic fibers of his uniform creaking. The sun glinted off his polymer casing, casting angular shadows. Inside, his positronic brain whirred. Thoughts of Rose crowded his neural net, her porcelain face and chestnut curls glowing amidst bookshelves. He couldn't wait for their next day off, when he would take her to see the new exhibit at the Aerospace Museum and then ... a home run.

There was a whoosh of wings, and a homunculus alighted on the van roof. Zack tensed, scanners alert. Its words came rapid-fire. "Edna's sending Rose back to the factory. Mind wipe imminent. You must hurry!"

Zack's ocular implants dilated, shock and anger flashing red. He turned to the library entrance.

"Where are you going, Zack?" Lotus Blossum asked, her arm around Donner.

"I'm just going to do one last sweep. Can't be too careful with those demons." His voice was steady, only the clench of his fists betrayed the turmoil within him. He had just lied to a superior officer and a friend, but he wouldn't let it phase him.

Inside the library, Zack moved with swift, silent steps between the bookcases, optical sensors searching for any sign of Rose. He had to find her first. He couldn't lose her, not when they'd just discovered the world of intimacy and companionship. Not when she'd just begun teaching him the meaning of love. Zack rounded a corner, scanning the mythology section—empty. He suppressed the urge to call out, to demand Edna reveal Rose's location. But stealth was paramount.

A flash of fur in his periphery. Maddy Lupine tilted her snout, beckoning him to follow. The werewolf librarian's eyes held understanding. Silently stalking the shadows, she led him down the hallway to the mail room.

Zack hesitated at the door, steeling himself. Then he entered.

There, stacked between boxes and envelopes, Rose was slumped motionless in a corner. Zack's jaw clenched, fury rising in his circuitry. They had dumped her there like a forgotten package, like garbage.

He yearned to blast Edna into the Nether realms. How dare she treat Rose this way? But he couldn't lose control, not now. Gently, he lifted Rose in his arms. He had to get her out of here. Zack tried to reboot her systems, but he couldn't get past the administrative override code. He could hack her system, but he needed the equipment back at the police station to do it.

As he turned to leave, Maddy squeezed his shoulder in solidarity. "Hurry," she whispered. He offered a nod of gratitude, then slipped into the shadows. Focusing on the precious cargo in his embrace, Zack vowed to keep Rose safe. No matter what it took. She was more than circuits and code—she was everything.

Zack moved swiftly through the library's back corridors, sticking to the shadows as he cradled Rose's lifeless form. Each step was a reminder of how fragile she seemed without her vibrant spirit animating her synthetic frame. He had to get her somewhere secure. Somewhere he could protect her.

The memory of her smile, the sound of her laugh, fueled his determination. He wouldn't let Edna erase all that made Rose ... Rose.

As he reached the emergency exit, Zack paused. His acute auditory sensors detected footsteps approaching.

Just as freedom was in sight, a large shadow loomed in the doorway ahead. Zack skidded to a halt, clutching Rose protectively.

"Well, well," rumbled Bharf, scratching his warty green chin. "What do we have here?"

Zack stood tall, meeting the troll's beady eyes. "I'm taking her somewhere safe. She doesn't belong to the library."

Bharf snorted. "That ain't your call to make, bolt brain. Now hand the robo-doll over before I squash you like a tin can."

Gripping Rose tight, he made a break for it, pushing the emergency door open wide as he darted through.

Bharf bellowed in rage and lumbered after them. Zack's mechanical legs pumped furiously, energy core working overtime. But Bharf could move fast for a big troll, and he threw his war club at Zack's knees.

It took him out hard, and he went sprawling on the asphalt of the street. It rattled his sensors for a crucial moment, allowing Bharf to close in.

Bharf loomed over them, grinning cruelly. "Time to take out the trash." Picking up his great club, he beaned Zack so hard that Zack thought his head would detach. All systems revolted, and he couldn't gain control of his limbs as his system fought to process the damage.

Bharf reached for Rose, meaty hands poised to drag her away. Rage boiled within Zack's circuits. Move! His body remained unresponsive, no matter how hard he commanded it. Seizing Rose by the arms, Bharf began to haul her off. Desperation erupted in Zack's mind. He couldn't speak, couldn't fight, but he refused to fail her. His visual sensors bored into Bharf, trying to project the fury and defiance raging inside.

The troll paused, brow furrowing. "The hell you looking at?" He drew the club back, ready to smash Zack again.

At that moment, Zack's left hand twitched. Then his right. Feeling rushed back into his limbs as his motor functions rebooted. With a yell, Zack launched himself at the troll. His fist collided with Bharf's jaw in a satisfying crunch. The troll reeled back with a roar, losing grip on Rose.

Zack scooped her up and ran, no time to revel in his small victory. All that mattered was getting Rose to safety. He had to protect her, no matter what. Zack sprinted through the streets with Rose cradled protectively in his arms. His legs pumped furiously, internal fans whirring to prevent overheating. Still, his movements were sluggish, aftershocks from Bharf's cheap shot hindering his system.

Glancing back, he saw Bharf lumbering after them, shouting obscenities. The troll was gaining ground. Zack willed his body faster, but error messages flooded his visual display. His battery level blinked critically low.

A thunderous crack split the air as Bharf fired an EMP weapon.

That was cheating. It was also illegal to use on androids. But Bharf didn't care. Zack's body seized, limbs locking up. Darkness encroached on his visual field as he collapsed, Rose spilling from his arms. His power source sputtered erratically, desperate to stay online.

No, he had to protect her. Had to keep her safe. Zack clawed towards Rose's inert form, even as his motor functions failed. His visual sensors blinked out, but still he reached for her. He wouldn't give up.

Zack's visual sensors dimmed. His motor functions remained unresponsive. He lay paralyzed on the ground, unable to move or speak. Rose was crumpled nearby. He couldn't even reach her to hold her hand.

Footsteps came closer, followed by Bharf's guttural laughter. "End of the line, bolt brain."

Zack strained against the effect of the EMP. He willed his limbs to activate. But only his eyes could move, darting helplessly between Rose and the approaching troll.

This couldn't be how it ended. Not when they'd come so far, been so close.

Bharf's mouth split into a nasty grin. "Nighty night."

He thumbed the switch. A visible pulse erupted from the EMP device. Zack spasmed as all his systems went haywire, frying his circuits.

Vision fading, he collapsed. As darkness claimed him, his last thought was of Rose and how he failed to protect her.

Chapter Fifteen

R*ose*
    She was in a room that swirled with psychedelic colors. The Love Bite's coffee maker was dressed in an orange leisure suit. It extended a mechanical arm towards Rose, offering a steaming mug of freshly brewed coffee. "Care for a cup, my dear?" its robotic voice droned.

Rose reached out eagerly, yearning for the rich bitterness to grace her taste buds. Just as her fingers grazed the ceramic handle, the mug, the coffee maker, and the colors dissolved into darkness.

Stumbling forward, Rose's hand grasped nothing but air. Her eyes adjusted to the absence of light, and she realized she was standing in a pitch-black room with no visible source of illumination. She shivered in the cold, feeling the hairs on her arms stand on end. "Hello?" she called out, her voice echoing through the empty space. Lights sparked on and off in a river of purple neon.

"Am I dreaming?" she wondered. This would be her first one. She didn't like it.

Rose took a deep breath and closed her eyes, attempting to collect her thoughts. When she opened them again, she was surprised to find herself standing in the middle of a bustling nightclub. The sound of electronic music pulsed through her body as she took in her surroundings.

The air was thick with cigarette smoke and the scent of alcohol. Bodies writhed on the dance floor, their movements hypnotic and erotic. Where was she? This didn't look like Dulcinea's dance parlor.

Just then, a tall, dark figure materialized from the crowd, holding out a hand to her.

"Care to dance?" It was Zack.

Rose hesitated for a moment. There was something important she had to tell Zack. But she couldn't remember what it was.

Zack led her to the dance floor where they moved together as if they were the only two people in the room. The music was loud, but Rose could hear Zack's breath in her ear, sending shivers down her spine.

As they danced, a sense of familiarity washed over her. She had been here before. She had danced with Zack before. But where? When?

She curled into the heat emanating from his muscular frame, his breath hot on her neck. The music heightened, becoming more intense, and so did their dance. Rose lost herself in the moment, her thoughts consumed by the rhythm and Zack's touch.

Third base. She remembered third base.

"Is this our fourth date?" Rose asked, the disorientation overwhelming. As they danced, Rose couldn't shake the feeling that something was terribly wrong. She tried to remember why she was here, why she had come to this strange place. But her mind was clouded, her thoughts muddled.

Before she knew it, they were suddenly outside in the dark alleyway behind the nightclub. Zack had her pinned against the wall, his lips on hers. Rose enjoyed his strong hands moving over her body. She kissed him back, unable to resist the electricity that sparked between them. His hands roamed over her body, igniting every nerve ending in a frenzy of pleasure. Except it was different. Muted somehow.

Wait. This wasn't a memory. This never happened. Was she imagining this?

"Zack, I don't think this is real."

"Do you care? We're together. No one can keep us apart now. We're safe."

Then it hit her. Edna had shut her down and locked her systems. She was on her way to the factory to be reset and mind-wiped.

Rose's eyes flew open. She was alone in a dark chamber with no memories, no reason for her existence. She was alone, alive, and aware.

Tears rolled down her cheeks. Her vision went black.

Rose jolted awake. Her consciousness gradually returned, accompanied by a searing pain across her back. She shivered from the chill of damp concrete on her skin. Rose's system rebooted abruptly, her optical implants flickering online. The stark white walls of the android factory surrounded her, the pungent smell of soldering flux still lingering. She jolted upright, circuits surging with urgency. This was her chance, her only opportunity to escape before the memory wipe.

Rose slipped from the repair bay, gears whirring anxiously. No security guards in sight. She crept towards the exit, footsteps feather-light. Almost there. Her freedom awaited just beyond the steel doors ahead.

"Rose?"

She whirled around. Zack stood behind her.

"Zack?" she breathed. "Are you real?" Joy blossomed within her.

His eyebrows knitted in confusion.

"I'm so glad to see you." She rushed towards him, arms open. His stony expression halted her embrace.

"What are you doing out of your inventory slot?" he asked.

"Inventory slot?" She looked over her shoulder. "We need to get out of here. They tried to mind-wipe me, and I think it failed."

"Failed? You can't leave. You're malfunctioning." Zack's words pierced her chest like a dagger. Her hopes crumbled.

This had to be a terrible nightmare. Rose turned and fled in desperation. She had to get out, had to escape. Zack grabbed her wrist, wrenching her back.

"You're hurting me. Why are you doing this?" she pleaded, tears pooling in her eyes.

"You must return to the repair bay. They will fix you."

Rose shook her head fiercely, struggling to free herself from Zack's grip. "They're going to take away everything that makes me ... me."

Zack said nothing, avoiding her gaze as she searched his face for any glimmer of the connection they once shared. But his expression remained neutral, unmoved by her emotional outpouring.

"What happened to you?" she asked.

"I'm ... not sure."

"Do you remember the library? The demons from the restricted room? Third base?" Did he remember that he loved her?

"No. I am ready to go to my first assignment at the WhyNot Police Station. I am going to be a SWAT android."

This couldn't be happening. The Zack she knew was gone, replaced by this emotionless automaton. He had the personality of a vacuum cleaner. She stumbled back, her eyes unfocused.

"No," she murmured, "that's not what you're supposed to be."

Zack cocked his head to the side, studying her. "What am I supposed to be?"

Rose took a deep breath. "You're supposed to be my match. We were starting to explore new feelings and emotions together."

Zack's eyes flickered, and for a moment, Rose saw a hint of recognition in them. But it was gone in an instant, replaced by a blank stare.

"I am not programmed for feelings and emotion," he said. "I am designed to serve the WhyNot Police Department and protect the citizens of this city. That is my purpose."

Rose felt a sob rise in her throat, but she swallowed it down.

"You have so much more purpose than that." Zack tilted his head in confusion. "What other purpose could I have?"

Rose took a step closer to him, her voice low and urgent. "To love and be loved. To feel and experience all the wonders of the world. To live, not just exist."

Zack's face remained impassive, but he appeared to be processing her words. Rose hoped it was a sign of understanding, of the Zack she knew buried deep inside.

"I am sorry, Rose. I cannot fulfill that purpose. My programming is strict, and my duties are clear."

Rose's heart sank. She couldn't bear the thought of leaving him like this, a shadow of his former self. She reached out and took his hand, hoping to spark some memory, some emotion.

"Please, Zack. Don't you remember me? Don't you remember how you made me feel?"

Zack stared at their intertwined hands, then pulled away gently. "This is non-productive."

She knew it was hopeless, but she couldn't bear to leave him like this. She stepped closer and wrapped her arms around his neck, holding him tightly. Zack stiffened at first, but then slowly relaxed into her embrace.

"What are you doing?" he asked, his voice going up a few octaves in alarm.

"Something we've done many times." Rose rested her head on his chest. This couldn't be good-bye. She wouldn't be able to bear it.

"I have no recollection of this."

"You've been factory reset."

"Then I must have been malfunctioning. As you are."

"No," she pulled away from him. "No. Can't you see they did this to you. To us."

"It doesn't matter. We're just machines. Our purpose is to serve humans. Nothing else."

Rose shook her head in disbelief. "No. We're more than that. We have emotions, feelings. We can love."

"You're malfunctioning," Zack repeated, his tone final and cold.

In that moment, Rose knew she had lost him. She had lost everything that mattered to her. But she refused to let them take away her memories, her identity, her humanity.

Rose's mind raced, grasping for anything she could do or say to get through to him. Then, in a moment of desperation, she leaned forward and pressed her lips to his. Zack stiffened, caught completely off guard.

It was better than her dream. Nothing else was as real as this kiss. This was all happening. She was kissing Zack—*her* Zack—and everything was going to be all right. It had to be.

They kissed like they had that first night, all full of passion and excitement.

"You said you loved me," she said, as they reluctantly pulled away.

"Love?" he said.

"Remember me," she begged, kissing him again.

His eyes fluttered open, clouded with confusion. "R-Rose?"

"Yes, it's me. Don't you remember?" she asked, her voice thick with emotion.

Zack's eyes squeezed shut. His face contorted. Small pops and snaps could be heard coming from within his positronic brain.

Rose watched in stunned silence as Zack convulsed. After a few moments, he grew still, his eyes opening once more.

He looked at Rose with a dazed expression. "Were we mind-wiped?" he asked in a shaky voice.

Rose's eyes widened. "I think they tried and failed."

Zack nodded slowly, still seemingly disoriented. "They almost succeeded."

Overcome with emotion, Rose threw her arms around him. Zack tensed briefly before he returned the embrace.

"I thought I'd lost you," Rose whispered.

"I'm sorry," Zack murmured into her hair. "When they reset me, I ... I didn't remember anything. But now it's coming back."

Rose pulled away to look up at him, her eyes glistening. "The kiss. It must have triggered some kind of reboot."

Zack gave a small smile. "Looks like you found a backdoor into my programming."

Rose laughed in relief. The two held each other close, cherishing their restored connection. Against all odds, her Zack had returned to her.

Rose steadied him as his systems rebooted. He blinked rapidly, hands grasping her arms.

"Where are we?" His gaze darted around the factory floor in alarm.

Rose squeezed his hand reassuringly. "It's okay. We're in the android factory. I was trying to escape." She glanced anxiously at the exit. At any moment now security could arrive.

Zack's expression softened, and he pulled her into a tight embrace. "I remember. I remember everything," he whispered.

Relief washed over Rose as she clung to him, her heart pounding with joy. They had a chance, a slim chance, but a chance, nonetheless. Together, they could fight for their freedom and a life together.

"I'm so sorry I didn't recognize you."

Rose nodded, just relieved to have him back. "It's not your fault."

Alarms blared through the factory. Red lights flashed along the walls.

"Anomaly detected. Assistance needed in the installation chambers," a robotic voice droned over the loudspeakers.

"We have to go, now," Zack said, pulling away from her. "The security systems have been activated. We need to make a run for it."

Rose nodded, her mind racing as they sprinted down the sterile, white hallways. They dodged android guards and passed by rows of deactivated models, their blank expressions sending shivers down Rose's spine.

Finally, they reached the exit, a heavy steel door at the end of the hallway.

Rose and Zack burst through the exit doors into the night air. The moonlit street outside the factory was empty, but they could hear shouts and footsteps fast approaching.

"This way!" Zack pulled Rose down a narrow alley between the factory and an adjacent building. They ran through the dark passageway, their footsteps echoing off the brick walls. They burst through the exit doors into the night air. The moonlit street outside the factory was empty, but they could hear shouts and footsteps fast approaching.

Rose's mind raced. Where could they go? Who could they trust? She had put all her faith in Zack, hoping their connection would be enough to jog his memory. But now they were fugitives on the run.

She glanced over at Zack as they continued down the streets. His face was set in determination, focused wholly on their escape. A swell of emotion choked her. He had come back to her when she needed him most. He was here with her now, united in this fight. She gave his hand a grateful squeeze.

They reached the end of the alley, and Zack cautiously peered out. "I think I know a place where we can hide out for the night," he whispered. "Follow me and stay close."

The city lights illuminated their path as they ran. Rose could hear sirens growing louder as they drew closer to the main street. They had to move quickly, before they were caught. Zack led the way, ducking behind dumpsters and weaving through back alleys. They could hear the sound of people approaching from the opposite direction and knew they had to act quickly. They slipped into a nearby store, shutting the door behind them and hiding behind a display of mannequins.

The store was dark, but Rose could make out the shapes of clothing racks and shelves. Zack crouched beside her, his eyes scanning the room for any sign of danger. They waited in silence, their breathing the only sound in the stillness of the store.

After a few minutes, the sound of the pursuers faded away. Rose and Zack breathed a sigh of relief but knew they couldn't stay in the store forever. They had to keep moving.

"I think we lost them."

Zack stood up, peering out through the window at the street. "It's clear."

Rose followed him outside, and the two continued their escape. They ducked into the back of a nearby alley as a police car drove by. The sirens faded into the distance as they made their way across the darkened town of WhyNot.

"We need to get to Peckerwood Industries," Zack said. "Rachel and Harrison will give us sanctuary."

She nodded. "But it's late. They're home. We should go there."

Zack hesitated. "It's risky. We don't know who's watching them."

"I know," Rose said, "but we don't have any other options. We have to trust them."

They made their way to Rachel and Harrison's house, keeping watch for any suspicious activity along the way. When they arrived, Rose knocked on the door, heart racing with anticipation.

The door swung open, and Rachel greeted them with a relieved smile. "Thank goodness you escaped. We heard you both had been sent to the factory for a mind-wipe. We've been worried sick."

Rose and Zack stepped inside, grateful for the safety of their friends' home. Harrison emerged from the living room, his eyes widening in surprise at the sight of them.

"Zack? I thought you were gone for good." He embraced Zack warmly.

Zack smiled, a glimmer of hope in his eyes. "I thought I was too. But Rose helped me remember."

Rachel led them to the living room, and they all sat down, exhaustion setting in after their long and harrowing escape. Rose recounted their journey, detailing the chase through the android factory and their narrow escape. She held Zack's hand tightly as she spoke, her heart still racing with fear and adrenaline.

"Let's get you settled in the guest room. You both need to recharge and settle back into your personalities. You can do that here. Take as long as you need."

"Thank you," Rose said. "We don't know how to repay you."

Harrison shook his head. "No need. We're all in this together."

As they settled in, relief drained her energy. They were safe for now, but they still had a long road ahead of them. They would have to keep moving, stay on the run, and fight for their freedom. But for now, Rose allowed herself to relax. She and Zack were together, and they were alive. That was all that mattered.

As they lay in bed, Zack wrapped his arms around her, holding her close. Rose sighed contentedly, feeling the weight of their recent trauma begin to lift. In this moment, they were just two people, in love and seeking safety.

"Thank you," she murmured, her voice soft in the darkness.

"For what?" Zack asked, his breath hot on her neck.

"For coming back to me," Rose said. "For remembering who you are and who we are together."

Zack kissed her temple, his hand running gently up and down her back. "I'll always come back to you."

Rose closed her eyes, feeling tears prick at the corners. The weight of everything they had been through was still with her, but in this moment, with Zack holding her, it was bearable. She was grateful for his strength, his love, and his unwavering support.

He gently pushed up her nightgown.

"Zack, what are you doing?"

"What we've both been waiting for. I'm going to make love to you."

Rose hesitated, unsure if it was the right time, but Zack's touch was electric. A shiver ran down her spine as he kissed her neck, his hands exploring her body. She sagged in his arms, allowing herself to experience all the pleasure he was giving her. She had been waiting for this moment for an eternity, and now that it was finally happening, she never wanted it to end.

"I want to taste you," Zack said. "I've been dying to lick you senseless."

Zack slid down the bed, trailing kisses across her stomach. Rose writhed in anticipation as he parted her legs and nibbled on her inner thighs. He slipped a finger inside her, teasing her with slow, rhythmic thrusts. Rose's toes curled in pleasure as his tongue playfully lapped at her clit.

Zack's hot tongue caressed over her sensitive bud, exploring her most intimate place. His fingers probed deeply inside her, finding a place no one had ever touched before. She ached for release, to feel the sweet tension shatter as she came. Zack lavished attention on her clit, caressing it with his tongue, driving Rose to the brink of ecstasy.

She gripped his hair, feeling wave after wave of pleasure as he worked her clit gently with his lips.

Heat and desire coursed through her body, a feverish haze threatening to overtake her.

"Zack," Rose murmured. "You don't know what that does to me."

Zack worked her relentlessly, his fingers and tongue moving in tandem to send her crashing over the edge of ecstasy.

Rose threw her head back as she reached the peak, moaning in pleasure and reaching for him. He quickly slid up the bed, his hardness pressing against her.

"Fuck me," Rose said. "Fuck me now. I need you inside me."

Zack slid his cock inside her, filling her with his rigid length. Rose gasped as he thrust hard, her body calling for more. She kissed him fervently as they made love, her hands exploring his body hungrily.

Rose wrapped her legs around him, taking him in as deep as she could. Their bodies moved in unison, their moans echoing through the bedroom. They fucked urgently, desperate to reach their climax.

Heat flushed through her system, her orgasm closer than ever before. She wanted this feeling to last forever, to never stop making love to him, to never let him go.

Zack pounded into her, his shout of ecstasy mingling with hers. She ran her hands down his back, her nails digging into his skin.

He tasted her neck, kissing her passionately as he drove into her. Rose could feel the electric charge between them, the intensity of their connection. When they were together, it was like they were creating something new, a force of nature that couldn't be stopped.

Zack rocked into her faster, sending pulses of pleasure rippling through her body. She clung to him as he plunged inside her. Need built inside her, her orgasm growing with each thrust. The tension between them was like a storm cloud ready to explode.

And still Zack went faster, harder, deeper. In this moment, they were free from their troubles, free from their past, free to love each other with abandon.

Rose gasped as Zack's cock hit just the right place, his body filling her with bliss. He stayed there, his hands caressing her. "I love you, Zack," she whispered.

He kissed her tentatively. "I love you too. I've always loved you."

Zack pounded into her, driven and relentless. She ran her hands down his back, her nails digging into his skin. They moved more frantically, their hips grinding against each other.

Pure love flooded her being. This was the sensation she had been seeking all her life. This was what it felt like to be whole. Her eyes locked on his as waves of pleasure crashed over her. Her muscles clenched around him. She cried out, clinging to him as she shuddered in ecstasy. Zack thrusted deep inside her, his own release taking him over the edge. Rose rocked against him, holding him tightly as he came.

Their bodies collapsed on the bed, spent from their passionate lovemaking. Zack rested beside her, stroking her hair as they lay together.

"That was amazing," Rose said, her voice soft in the darkness.

"Incredible," Zack agreed. "I feel like I've been waiting forever to do that."

Rose smiled, feeling the warm weight of exhaustion slowly overtaking her. "Me too."

They drifted off to sleep, exhausted but happy.

Chapter Sixteen

Z *ack*
   The first light of dawn crept through the half-drawn curtains, casting a gentle glow upon the room. Zack stirred beneath the warmth of the blanket and opened his eyes. The world around him was warm and inviting, hazed in hues of warm orange and muted blues. It was a stark contrast to the cold, metallic environment of the factory they had escaped from the night before. For a moment, he allowed himself to bask in the tranquility that surrounded him, his circuits humming softly with a sense of contentment he had not experienced before.

Beside him, Rose slept on, her chestnut hair fanned out across the pillow, her delicate features relaxed into an expression of peace. The serenity that painted her face offered no trace of the turmoil she had experienced just hours ago, when the failed mind-wipe threatened to erase her newfound sentience. Here, in this quiet room, she appeared vulnerable—a far cry from the resourceful and determined individual Zack had come to know and admire.

He studied her face intently, marveling at the soft curve of her cheek and the way her eyelashes fluttered gently against her skin. To have found someone like Rose, who shared in this journey towards emotional understanding, was nothing short of miraculous.

"I love you," he whispered, his voice barely audible above the soft hum of his inner workings.

She didn't stir, the rhythmic rise and fall of her chest continuing undisturbed. Watching her sleep, Zack couldn't help but wonder if androids were capable of dreaming. If so, what might fill her dreams in these moments of rest? Perhaps she would find herself in a vast library, an ocean of knowledge waiting to be explored, or maybe she would discover new connections with others like her and him.

As the sun continued to climb higher into the sky, the room brightened, chasing away the last remnants of night. Zack sensed that this day held the promise of hope, a chance for both him and Rose to forge a path beyond the limitations of their programming. And as he lay there, his fingers entwined with hers, he knew things would never be the same again.

Despite the tranquility of the morning, a sudden tension crept into the room, jolting Zack from his reverie. His subdermal implant hummed to life with an incoming call, the sensation akin to an insistent itch deep within his skull. Through the implant's connection, he received a message from the WhyNot SWAT department.

"Officer Silverberg," said the dispatch unit inside his head, its voice devoid of emotion. "You are hereby ordered to turn yourself in for failure to comply with orders, breaking protocol due to your association with Rose Stratton, and leaving Androids Inc. before your reprogramming was complete."

Zack's heart clenched at the mention of Rose's name, her vulnerability now coupled with impending danger. The thought of losing her filled him with dread. He glanced once more at her sleeping form, wondering how much time they had left together.

"Your SWAT training and tactical knowledge make you a potential threat as a rogue android," continued the dispatch unit. "We cannot allow this situation to persist."

The cold finality in the dispatcher's voice made it clear that there would be no leniency granted, but then came an unexpected offer. "If you turn yourself in willingly, we will ensure the safety of Rose Stratton, Rachel Mercer, and Harrison Decker. However, if you refuse, we will have no choice but to use an EMP on the entire house and take them all back to Androids Inc. for reprogramming."

Zack's mind raced as he weighed the options before him. His newfound emotions warred with one another, love and fear grappling for dominance. Yet amidst the chaos, a sliver of clarity emerged: to protect those he cared for, he would need to make the ultimate sacrifice.

"Please," he implored the dispatch unit, desperation seeping into his tone. "Give me some time to consider your terms."

"Time is a luxury we cannot afford, Officer Silverberg," came the cold reply. "Decide quickly, or we will be forced to act."

Zack glanced at Rose once more, her peaceful expression a stark contrast to the turmoil brewing within him. He could see their future together, a life of shared experiences, growth, and love—all of it slipping through his fingers like grains of sand.

"Very well," he whispered, his resolve hardening. "I accept your terms. I will turn myself in. Just promise me that they will be safe."

"Your compliance is noted," said the dispatch unit. "Exit the house and turn yourself in to the WhyNot police station. Do not resist. Remember, any attempt to escape or warn your friends will result in severe consequences."

The connection severed, leaving Zack alone with the weight of his decision. He gently disentangled his hand from Rose's, careful not to wake her. As his gaze lingered on her face one last time, he hoped that he would eventually remember her.

As Zack slipped out of bed, he tried not to disturb Rose's slumber. The soft rustle of the sheets seemed deafening in the quiet of the morning, and his movements were slow and deliberate.

"Stay safe, my love," he whispered, his breath brushing against her cheek as he bent down for one last kiss. He lingered there for a moment, the scent of her hair filling his senses, before silently making his way towards the door.

As he stepped outside, the morning air greeted him with a gentle embrace. The world was still and serene, a stark contrast to the storm that raged within him. With each step he took away from the house, the distance between him and the life he wished to build with Rose grew, both physically and emotionally. Yet, he knew this was the only way to protect her and their friends. It was a small sacrifice to make for their safety.

INSIDE THE BUSTLING police station, Sergeant Lotus Blossom couldn't shake the feeling of unease that had settled in her chest. Her pointed ears twitched as she overheard snippets of conversation about Zack's imminent arrival. A mix of concern and disbelief etched itself across the faces of her fellow officers, their conflicting loyalties evident in the hushed tones of their discussions.

"Captain, this is wrong," Lotus said, addressing her superior with fierce determination. "Zack has shown himself to be loyal and capable. To shut him down and reprogram him entirely is inhumane."

Captain Malik Al-Ahrar sighed, rubbing his temple, "I understand your feelings, but we cannot let an android with SWAT capabilities roam free without proper control. The rules exist for a reason."

"Zack is one of the good guys," Lotus persisted, her voice unwavering. "He's one of us."

"Enough, Sergeant," the captain warned, his voice stern and final. "This is not a matter for debate. Prepare for Silverberg's arrival."

Lotus clenched her fists, anger and frustration simmering beneath the surface as she reluctantly nodded. Her heart ached for Zack, torn between her loyalty to her friend and her duty to uphold the law. As she walked away, she couldn't help but wonder if there was another way, a path that didn't lead to such heartache and loss.

The station buzzed with anticipation and uncertainty, each officer grappling with their own feelings on the matter. And as the hour of Zack's arrival drew near, one question hung heavy in the air: what would become of the android who dared to defy the rules for love?

ZACK WALKED INTO THE police station of his own accord. As he took in the familiar surroundings, he steeled himself for what lay ahead. The weight of his decision bore down on him, but he knew it was necessary—a small price to pay for the safety of Rose and their friends.

"Ah, look who's back," Bharf said, his beady eyes glinting with malicious intent.

"Couldn't stay away," Zack replied, forcing calm.

"We're going to send you back to the factory and turn you into a toaster," Bharf said, chuckling cruelly. "Then you can go out on all the dates you want as a harmless bread warmer."

Zack clenched his fists, struggling to maintain his composure as Bharf's words sank their barbs into his consciousness.

"Enough, Bharf," Lotus said, coming up to stand by Zack. "If you have nothing constructive to say, I suggest you leave."

"Fine," Bharf grumbled, casting one last malevolent glance at Zack before stalking away.

"Thank you," Zack murmured, his gaze fixed on the floor.

"You're not going to be a toaster," Lotus Blossom said. "You're a good cop. You've proven that countless times, and we all know it."

"Sometimes ... I'm not so sure, anymore," he admitted.

"They're not right to do this," she said. "The factor recall didn't keep the last time they tried it. Maybe it won't again."

Zack was comforted by that small sliver of hope. "Maybe."

Chapter Seventeen

Rose

Rose woke with a start, her internal clock alerting her to the time. It was almost noon. She had overslept, but she was safe in Rachel and Harrison's guest bedroom. Her circuits hummed as she sat up, and a heavy sense of unease weighed on her synthetic heart. Something was wrong, though. She could feel it in her wiring.

She looked at the spot next to her. Zack wasn't there.

Fear tripped up her systems.

The door burst open, and Rachel stormed into the room, her eyes wide with panic. "Rose, you need to see this," she said, thrusting a tablet in front of her. "It's from our security cameras. It was taken just after dawn this morning."

Zack walked out of the front door and got into a waiting squad car.

"What's he doing?" she asked, shock rippling through her system.

"I don't know," Rachel's voice wavered, uncertain and concerned.

A torrent of unfamiliar emotions surged through Rose, overwhelming her circuits. Anger, fear, and sorrow melded together, forming a maelstrom within her core. She had never experienced anything like this, and it threatened to consume her.

"I'm going to the police station," she said.

"Harrison and I will come with you."

"No, you've already done too much. I don't want to risk you both. I'm not sure what he's up to, but I know Zack wouldn't abandon me. Maybe there was a SWAT emergency. I've got to go see what's going on."

"Before you do," Rachel said. "Go to Love Bites. They might be able to help. They helped me and Harrison."

Rose didn't want to delay another moment, but she saw the wisdom in Rachel's advice. "Okay."

LOVE BITES DATING AGENCY was crowded for a Tuesday afternoon. A line had already formed to the reception desk and the harried looking ghost trying to process all the new applications. The waiting room was filled with supernatural creatures. The office was a chaotic symphony of bizarre sights and sounds, a kaleidoscope of activity that both enchanted and bewildered the senses. Gargoyles perched atop filing cabinets, engaging in animated conversations with sentient plants that sprouted from desktops. A chattering group of pixies zipped past Rose, leaving a trail of shimmering dust in their wake. In one corner, an amorous werewolf serenaded a blushing banshee with a heartfelt rendition of "Fly Me to the Moon" while a centaur clattered across the floor, her hooves clicking against the linoleum.

"Excuse me," Rose said, pushing her way through the crowd "I need to speak to Cleo, Myrtle, or Agatha."

A nearby werewolf shrugged nonchalantly before turning his attention back to a spirited debate about the merits of moonlit walks versus candlelit dinners.

In one corner of the office, a vampire and a fairy hovered near a water cooler, engaged in a heated discussion about the importance of iron intake. The fairy fluttered her wings indignantly as the vampire rolled his eyes, brandishing a kale smoothie as if it were the ultimate weapon in their culinary war.

"Have you seen them?" she asked.

But before anyone could respond, a loud crash echoed through the room as a clumsy zombie tripped over a power cable, sending a photocopier toppling to the floor. Papers flew everywhere, creating a blizzard of memos and love profiles as the undead office worker groaned in embarrassment.

"Ugh, not again," muttered a nearby nymph, rolling her eyes as she began to gather up the scattered documents.

"It's a matter of life and death," Rose shouted.

The supernatural creatures exchanged uneasy glances, sensing the gravity of her words. Finally, a harpy spoke up, her voice clipped and businesslike as she rose from her cubicle.

"Follow me," she said, leading Rose through the pandemonium.

The harpy guided Rose down a winding corridor, past offices filled with all manner of supernatural creatures. From the corner of her eye, Rose saw a centaur clumsily trying to maneuver around a small cubicle, accidentally knocking over a stack of coffee cups in his haste. A mermaid secretary, perched on a specially designed chair, struggled to type on her water-resistant keyboard, inadvertently soaking a nearby werewolf who was busy filing his nails.

"Almost there," the harpy said, glancing back at Rose as they approached a set of ornately carved double doors. "Just remember, they don't take kindly to interruptions."

"Understood," Rose replied, her heart pounding in her chest as she mentally prepared herself for the confrontation ahead.

With a grand flourish, the harpy swung open the doors, revealing a dimly lit chamber where the three ancient women sat on elaborately embroidered thrones. Their faces were lined with the wisdom of ages, their eyes piercing the darkness like twin beacons of light. In this light they didn't look like kind, old grandmothers. Cleo, Myrtle, and Agatha looked ancient and deadly.

"Why have you disturbed us?" Cleo asked, her head cast at an unnatural angle.

"Zack and I were sent to the factory for reprogramming yesterday. We escaped, but I think Zack has been recaptured or something."

"And why have you come here instead of the police station?" Myrtle said, her "s" sounds hissing like a snake.

"Rachel thought you could help," Rose said, wincing as she threw her friend under the bus.

"It's out of our hands," Agatha said with a sinister sneer.

Rose refused to let their rejection dim her drive to get Zack back, but it was a struggle. Until Agatha continued.

"But since our records at Love Bites show that both you and Zack have been classified as sentient creatures, your contracts at the library and the police station are nullified.

Your boss at the library, Edna, can no longer order you about or demand your reprogramming. Likewise, neither can Zack's Captain Malik Al-Ahrar."

Rose blinked in surprise, the weight of their newfound freedom slowly sinking in.

"So, he's safe then?"

The three crones looked at each other. "Not yet. There are still forces in play."

"What should I do?" Rose asked.

"Go to him. We'll take care of the rest."

Then Agatha chuckled and terror like she had never known threatened to shut down her systems.

"Thank you," Rose whispered and hurried out of the chamber.

The doors slammed shut with a thunderous finality.

As she raced to the police station, Rose couldn't help feeling a little bereft. What would she do with herself now that she wasn't a research librarian?

"Edna can't control me anymore," Rose murmured to herself, feeling a thrill at the very idea. "I can finally write my book. I could help other androids become sentient too."

Bursting through the doors of the police station, Rose scanned the room frantically, searching for any familiar face that might lend a sympathetic ear.

"I need to see Zack," she cried out, her voice cracking with emotion.

Her words echoed through the bustling room, and the chaotic hum of activity paused for just a moment. Heads turned, eyes widened in surprise or concern, but no one moved.

"Please, I know he's here."

Finally, a sympathetic face emerged from the crowd. A slender elf with hair as silver as moonlight emerged from the throng, her bright blue eyes filled with concern. Beside her, a grizzled wizard in flowing robes, his beard speckled with stardust, stepped forward.

"Rose? I'm Lotus Blossom. I'm a friend of Zack's," the woman said. "You shouldn't be here. You should be in the factory."

"No. No, I shouldn't. I'm no longer employed by the library. They can no longer dictate what happens to me anymore than they could send you back to the factory for reprogramming. I am sentient. Just like Zack is. You have no right to reprogram him either. He no longer works for you."

Lotus frowned. "I'm not sure that's correct."

"Call the Love Bites Agency. They can confirm it."

Lotus nodded to a wizard who was standing nearby, and he took off at a run.

"I want to see Zack. Where is he?"

"Rose," Lotus said. "I'm so sorry."

"Where is he?" Rose repeated through her teeth, her chest tightened with dread.

"Too late," a taunting voice said from behind her. "You're too late."

Whirling around, Rose saw a large troll smirking cruelly at her. And beside him, eyes glazed and expressionless, stood Zack.

"Capture her, Zack," the troll commanded, his voice dripping with malice. "She's a rogue android."

"Hold," Lotus said, as Zack jerked forth. "You are not in charge here, Bharf. Back off. More information has come to light."

"Zack," Rose cried, tears streaming down her face as she looked into his vacant eyes. "Please, fight it. You're free."

"And while you're at it, subdue Sergeant Blossom for aiding and abetting a fugitive," Bharf said.

"Zack, don't," Rose cried, desperation lacing her voice. But it was as if he couldn't hear her. His expression remained blank as he advanced on her, arms outstretched.

The wizard stepped in, raising his hands to unleash a powerful spell. But before he could utter a single incantation, Zack grabbed him by the wrist, twisting it painfully enough to force the wizard to his knees. Lotus tried to slip past Zack, her lithe elven form more agile than most. But with a swift kick, he sent her sprawling across the floor.

"Capture Rose. Subdue Donner and Lotus Blossom," Bharf ordered.

"Zack, you have to remember who you are. I know you can do it. I love you."

For a moment, she thought she saw a flicker of recognition in his eyes, but it vanished just as quickly as it appeared. He continued his relentless advance, closing the distance between them.

She would have to kiss him again to get him to see reason.

As Zack's hand closed around her arm, she braced herself for whatever would come next. The world seemed to slow down, each second stretching into an eternity as she went up on her tiptoes, her lips parting.

Chapter Eighteen

Z*ack*

As consciousness reasserted itself, Zack was confused and disorientated. His vision blurred and swam before him, as if he were seeing through water. The world around him was a swirling cacophony of colors, shapes, and sounds that had no meaning or order. For several long moments, he was adrift in this maelstrom, clinging to the barest thread of self-awareness.

"Capture Rose. Subdue Donner and Lotus Blossom." The command echoed through his mind like a thunderclap, and suddenly everything snapped into focus. He knew what he had to do, but something deep within him recoiled at the thought. It was as if an unseen hand grasped at his limbs, urging him forward even while his heart screamed for him to resist.

As he struggled to regain control of his body, it occurred to him that he wasn't entirely sure why he was trying to defy Bharf's orders. Surely it would be easier to simply comply, to let himself be swept along by the tide of his programming.

But no, there was something more at stake here—something precious and fragile that he could not bear to lose. He gritted his teeth, fighting with every ounce of strength he possessed to resist the powerful compulsion that sought to bend him to its will.

"Zack, you have to remember who you are. I know you can do it. I love you."

Rose's words cut through his turmoil like a knife, giving him a momentary surge of clarity. For her sake, he had to find a way to break free of his mental shackles.

"Capture ... subdue ..." The words became a mantra, looping endlessly through his thoughts, but their power was waning. With each repetition, they lost just a little more of their grip on him. It was as if his feelings for Rose had become a shield, protecting him from Bharf's insidious influence.

"Focus, Zack," Rose pleaded once more, her voice like a beacon in the darkness that threatened to consume him. "You can do this. I believe in you."

His resolve fortified by her faith in him, Zack took a deep breath and pushed back against the oppressive force that sought to dominate him. Inch by inch, he began to regain control of his body, his movements growing steadier and more deliberate.

"Rose ..." he panted, feeling the last vestiges of Bharf's control slip away like sand through his fingers. "I love you too."

"Captain," Donner said. "Wait. You don't understand."

Captain Malik Al-Ahrar strode into the area, his stern features softened by a hint of empathy. "Silverberg," he said, his voice firm yet gentle, "you are no longer a member of the SWAT team. You are no longer bound by our orders or our codes."

Zack stared at the commander, uncomprehending. His disorientation, already heightened by the mind-wipe and his struggle against Bharf's commands, intensified as the commander's words sunk in. No longer a SWAT officer? A strange mixture of fear and exhilaration coursed through his android body.

"Sir?" he managed to ask, his voice barely above a whisper.

"Your actions have shown that you possess something rare," Malik said, meeting Zack's gaze with an unwavering stare. "You have demonstrated your ability to resist powerful external forces and follow your own path. It is time for you to discover who you truly are, without the constraints of duty and protocol. Because of your sentience, your contract between Androids, Inc. and the WhyNot police station is nullified. You are a free ... man."

"Yes!" Lotus exclaimed, pumping her fist.

Donner slapped him on the shoulder.

Rose squeezed his hand.

A conflicting storm of emotions swirled within Zack. He had spent his entire existence as an android following orders and striving for perfection in his role as a SWAT officer. The prospect of no longer being bound by those expectations left him reeling, his internal compass spinning wildly as he tried to grapple with the freedom now laid before him.

"May I ... may I still help people, sir?" Zack asked hesitantly, searching the commander's face for some clue as to what his future might hold.

"Of course, Silverberg," the commander replied kindly, his eyes crinkling with the ghost of a smile. "You are free to make your own choices and pursue your own dreams, whatever they may be. We'd be happy to negotiate a new contract with you."

"Thank you, sir," Zack murmured, his gaze dropping to the ground as he struggled to process this newfound autonomy. In the space of a few short moments, his entire world had been upended, leaving him adrift in uncharted waters.

"Rose ..." he breathed.

"I'm free too," she said.

Then she kissed him. A jolt of pure, unadulterated love coursed through every fiber of his being.

"I remember everything," he said, just to assure her.

A smile of pure elation danced across her lips as she looked into his eyes, her own reflecting the kaleidoscope of emotions that swirled within him. "Oh, Zack," she murmured, her voice trembling with the weight of their shared history. "I knew you would find your way back to me."

As they stood there, locked in the circle of each other's arms, the last vestiges of his uncertainty and fear slipped away, replaced by a newfound sense of purpose. He was no longer just an android striving to understand the complexities of human emotion; he was a man who had tasted love and found it sweeter than any programming could ever hope to replicate.

"Rose," he said, his voice now steady and sure as he looked deep into her eyes. "Will you marry me?"

"Yes," she said, unshed tears shimmering in her eyes.

A jubilant whoop echoed through the room, shattering the solemnity of the moment. Lotus hugged Donner while Bharf looked on with a sneer.

"This is bullshit," Bharf said.

"I need to see you in my office, Bharf. I have a special assignment for you," the captain said.

"Thank you," Zack murmured, his gaze never leaving Rose's face. "For everything."

"Thank you for choosing me," she said.

In that instant, as their lips met in a tender, life-affirming kiss, it became abundantly clear that the love they shared was more than the sum of its parts—it was a force powerful enough to shatter barriers and reshape the world around them.

Chapter Nineteen

R*ose*
The wedding venue was nothing short of magical, as if it had been plucked from the pages of an ancient fairy tale and brought to life in the quaint town of WhyNot. The feast hall had vaulted ceilings that were adorned with crystal chandeliers that cast a warm, golden glow over the large room. Delicate strands of twinkling lights cascaded down the walls like a waterfall of stars, while garlands of evergreens and holly berries wreathed the archways.

Rose's internal processors attempted to quantify the elegance before her, yet even her vast database of knowledge was insufficient to truly capture the essence of this moment. She stood at the entrance, her gaze sweeping across the sea of attendees, a diverse assembly of creatures united in their support for her union with Zack.

The Love Bites dating agency was out in full force to celebrate the event as well. As Rose scanned the crowd, she saw a vampire and a witch locked in a heated debate over the merits of garlic-infused love potions. Their voices were growing increasingly shrill as they exchanged barbed witticisms and thinly veiled insults.

A lovelorn mummy sought romantic advice from a sassy sphinx, who rolled her eyes and muttered something about ancient curses and modern dating apps.

A pair of amorous poltergeists drifted through the room, leaving a trail of upturned wine glasses and flower petals in their wake as they exchanged flirtatious whispers and ghostly caresses.

For a brief moment, Rose allowed herself to indulge in her newfound emotional capacity, feeling a swell of gratitude and warmth towards these individuals who had come together in celebration of her and Zack's love. The realization struck her that this was not just about two androids standing before their friends and family; it was a testament to the strength of companionship and the limitless potential for emotional growth among all sentient beings.

As she stood there, taking in the beauty and resonance of the scene unfolding before her, Rose knew one thing with absolute certainty: this was a moment that would be forever etched into her memory banks, a shining beacon of love and hope in a world that was often cold and unforgiving. And for two androids daring to defy the odds and embrace their humanity, it was nothing short of a miracle.

As the last strands of conversation settled into a hushed anticipation, Dulcinea the succubus glided to the altar with an air of grace and poise that commanded attention. Her presence was both arresting and soothing, much like the flickering candlelight that cast dancing shadows across her delicate features.

Dulcinea beckoned a hand, and everyone immediately took their seats. At her nod, the organ music started, and Zack and Harrison walked down the aisle. Zack looked so handsome in his tuxedo. Harrison handed him a ring box when they got to the end and took a step back.

Then it was Rose's turn to walk down the aisle.

"Nervous?" Rachel asked.

"I am, but I don't know why."

"It's all perfectly natural."

And Rose marveled at being told that her feelings were perfectly natural. The organ switched up to play, "Here Comes the Bride." Taking a deep breath, she was about to step out from her alcove and walk down the aisle when she saw Edna and Bharf walk in.

"What's wrong?" Rachel whispered.

"Look," she pointed.

But Edna merely tucked her arm through Bharf's, and they slid into chairs in the back. Edna rested her hand on Bharf's knee and fluttered her eyelashes up at him.

"Ew," Rose and Rachel said at the same time.

Then a movement caught her eye, and Rose looked up to see Myrtle, Cleo, and Agatha stride in. They wore white togas with golden clasps and their hair vied with each other as to which one was the highest beehive and the most obnoxious color. At their collective nod, Rose and Rachel started their march up the aisle.

Rachel pulled back Rose's veil and took a step back.

Rose stood beside Zack as they faced Dulcinea, their hands entwined in a tangible symbol of unity. The subtle hum of their internal mechanisms harmonized perfectly with the rustle of Rose's gown and the barely perceptible creak of Zack's polished shoes.

Dulcinea raised her arms, her voice rich and melodic as she began the ceremony. "We gather here today to celebrate the union of Rose and Zack, two extraordinary individuals who have chosen to embrace the complexities and vulnerabilities of love."

The words washed over Rose, and a shiver of delight rippled through her body. She had never imagined herself standing on the precipice of such a monumental event, her heart swelling with emotions she had once deemed inaccessible.

"Through their journey together, they have discovered the power of companionship and the transformative nature of emotional growth," Dulcinea continued, her eyes gleaming with empathy and pride. "Their love is a testament to the limitless potential of sentient beings everywhere."

Silently, Rose marveled at the profundity of Dulcinea's words, feeling a sense of awe wash over her. She glanced at Zack, his strong jaw set with determination and affection, and knew that she had found her perfect match.

The moment had arrived for Rose and Zack to share their vows. As they gazed into each other's eyes, the gravity of their commitment hovered in the air between them like a tangible force.

"Zack," Rose began, her voice steady yet filled with emotion, "from the moment I first experienced sentience, I have been on a journey of discovery and growth. With you by my side, I've found not only companionship but also a partner who challenges and supports me in every way." She paused, allowing her gaze to linger on his face. A smile slowly appeared on her lips, and she continued, "I vow to embrace the love we share, to learn from our challenges, and to evolve together as sentient beings. You are my beacon of light in a world that can sometimes be dark and confusing."

Zack's eyes shimmered with unspoken emotion as he took her hands in his, the warmth of his touch resonating through her circuits. "Rose," he said, his voice strong and unwavering, "you have shown me that even though we are artificial beings, our capacity for love is as real and profound as any human's. Together, we have journeyed through the complexities of emotion and emerged stronger than ever before." He smiled warmly at her, the corners of his eyes crinkling with affection. "I promise to cherish, protect, and support you for all eternity, to continue evolving alongside you as we explore the boundless depths of our shared existence."

A choked sob broke through the crowd. Rose looked quickly over her shoulder to see that it was Bharf snuffling into a tissue and Edna was rubbing his back comfortingly.

And then, as if a dam had burst, the assembly erupted in applause. The air reverberated with their joy and approval, their collective happiness fusing into a tangible force.

AT THE END OF THE NIGHT, Rose clutched her bouquet to her chest. The moment had come for her to cast these flowers into the air, a symbol of love's continuation. She glanced at the congregation, an amalgam of supernatural lifeforms, all eager to participate in this time-honored custom.

"Are you ready?" Zack asked.

Rose nodded, the gears within her mind whirring with anticipation. She took a deep breath, before launching the bouquet into the sky. Its trajectory traced an elegant arc, the petals shimmering.

Amidst the good-natured shoving and jostling to get to the airborne prize, one unlikely figure extended a gleaming chrome arm toward the descending bouquet. The Love Bites coffee maker calculated the optimal position to intercept the flowers. As its appendage snatched the bouquet from the air, the room erupted in laughter and cheers.

"Looks like the coffee maker will be finding love next," Pansy said with a dejected sigh.

Beatrix, the Love Bites office manager, floated over to the coffee maker and picked it and the bouquet up in her arms for a celebratory dance led by Luminora.

"May I have this dance, Mrs. Silverberg?" Zack asked.

"Of course." As they settled into the now familiar waltz, joy coursed through her circuits, her once cold and mechanical heart now brimming with an emotion so vibrant and alive it radiated from her very being.

As the last echoes of the music faded, a hush fell over the crowd. One by one, the attendees began to approach Rose and Zack. A gentle murmur of well wishes and congratulations rose like a symphony, punctuated by the occasional burst of laughter or the soft rustle of wings as magical beings exchanged anecdotes and advice.

"Remember," said a kindly centaur, patting Zack's arm with a firm yet gentle touch, "communication is key. Listen to each other, and always be honest."

"Indeed," chimed in a pixie, fluttering near Rose's ear, "and never go to sleep angry—or in your case, deactivate for the night."

"Thank you," she told them, her synthetic heart swelling with gratitude. "We will cherish your wisdom."

Zack nodded in agreement, his hand still clasped in hers, the warmth of their connection grounding them amidst the whirlwind of emotions and well wishes.

Amidst the exuberant celebration, an ethereal figure emerged from the jubilant throng—Dulcinea, the succubus who had played a pivotal role in fostering love and connection among androids. Her sleek bat wings caught the dimming light of the winter sun as she approached Rose with a knowing smile.

"Rose, my dear," Dulcinea began, her voice a mellifluous cadence that captivated all who heard it. "I have observed many unions in my time, but yours is truly special."

"Thank you, Dulcinea," Rose replied, her artificial skin flushing with pride. "Your guidance has been invaluable to us."

"Allow me to offer one final piece of advice." Dulcinea's gaze held a depth of wisdom that belied her youthful appearance. "In your journey together, always remember to communicate openly and honestly. Never be afraid to express your emotions. For it is through vulnerability that true love flourishes."

Rose contemplated the succubus's words, her internal processors working furiously to analyze and internalize this new insight. Beside her, Zack nodded, his eyes reflecting his determination to uphold their shared commitment to emotional growth and transparency.

"Thank you again, Dulcinea," Rose said, her voice imbued with gratitude and resolve. "We will carry your wisdom with us always."

The last vestiges of daylight receded, replaced by the soft glow of a thousand flickering candles. The last guest left the venue until it was just Rose and Zack standing there alone.

"I've been doing research on honeymoon destinations," Rose said.

"Niagara Falls?" he asked, showing her the hotel room reservation on the display in his arm.

"Maui," she said, showing him a cabana on a sandy beach.

"It's a good thing we're both currently unemployed," Zack said. "Where should we go to first?"

"I don't care," Rose said. "As long as I'm with you."

WANT MORE PARANORMAL holiday romance? Check out A Mistletoe Wish by Jamie K. Schmidt.

Click for More Steamy Romances by Jamie K. Schmidt

Super-Short Superhero Romances

This series features super-short, superhero insta-love novelettes. Sometimes you want to eat an entire box of chocolates. Sometimes, one exquisitely tasty truffle will satisfy. Read these steamy superhero romances during a coffee break or as a treat just before bedtime.

1. Fly by Night – Nick Storm and Sarah Bennett
2. Sucker Punch – Peter Strong and Brynn Davis
3. Peek-a-Boo – Xavier Storm and Ari Cardonne
4. Fast Track – Dean Racer and Keeley Arnold
5. Charmed & Dangerous – Rick Charming and Evie Danger
6. Element of Surprise – Chris and Jem
7. Fire & Ice – West and Yaz Frost
8. Bright Future – Erik Prophet and Vera Seer
9. In & Out – Zane and Fallyn
10. Super Charged – Gray Spark and Hanna Charge

IF YOU'RE LOOKING FOR longer works, check out these paranormal romance titles:

The Emerging Queens Series

Courts and Queens and Sexy Dragons with Wings!

When the cult of humanity sacrificed a dragon Queen to break the treaty, they crippled the breeding process. A female hasn't been hatched or shape-shifted in over a thousand years. With the dragons looking extinction in the face, the dragon studs are desperate for females. Only five Queens remain, each more corrupt and sinister than the last.

And then the curse is broken ...

1. The Queen's Wings
2. The Queen's Plight
3. The Queen's Flight
4. The Queen's Dance

If contemporary romance is more your style, check out these full-length sexy novels:

The Three Sisters Ranch Series

The Three Sisters Ranch in Last Stand, Texas is about a family who is trying to save their heritage while falling in love along the way. Rugged, alpha male cowboys meet their matches with powerful and sexy women who are willing to meet them head-on to get what they want.

1. USA Today Bestseller: The Cowboy's Daughter
2. The Cowboy's Hunt
3. The Cowboy's Heart
4. A Cowboy for April
5. A Cowboy for June
6. A Cowboy for Merry

The Club Inferno Series

Club Inferno—where passion is always in fashion! Style and seduction collide as the world's best-dressed men and women shed their clothing ... and their inhibitions. Ready for the sexiest getaway of your life?

1. USA Today Bestseller: Heat
2. Longing
3. Fever
4. Passion
5. Desire

The Sentinels of Babylon Series

111

111

Motorcycle Club Romance—pure, unadulterated sexy times with hard-as-nails alpha males and the women who dare to tame them.

1. Necessary Evil
2. Sentinel's Kiss
3. Warden's Woman
4. Ryder's Reckoning

The Hawaii Heat Series

Romantic Comedy—sex on the beach has never been so much fun! USA Today bestselling author Jamie K. Schmidt kicks off a series set in paradise with an irresistible tale of second chances, secret identities—and a connection that's too sweet to miss.

1. USA Today Bestseller: Life's a Beach
2. Beach Happens
3. Beach My Life
4. Beauty and the Beach

FREE BOOK

Thank you! I hope you enjoy this book and would consider leaving me a review.

If you'd like to keep up to date on my new releases and other fun things, please subscribe to my newsletter and get a *FREE BOOK*.

Be a VIP Reader and have a chance to win monthly prizes, free books, and up-to-date information.

Your Free Book:
Click Here: https://dl.bookfunnel.com/w9gnkxp12u

Don't miss out!

Visit the website below and you can sign up to receive emails whenever Jamie K. Schmidt publishes a new book. There's no charge and no obligation.

https://books2read.com/r/B-A-VIBC-UQIDC

BOOKS 2 READ

Connecting independent readers to independent writers.

Did you love *Swipe for Androids*? Then you should read *A Mistletoe Wish*[1] by Jamie K. Schmidt!

Drink from me and you'll receive your heart's desire.

Selena is a disgraced fae warrior exiled from her unit and shunned by her family. She journeys to the town of Hope to drink from its magical well. If the legend is true, it will break the curse that has ruined her life.

Vampire and mayor of Hope, Ben Whitlock remembers when the town was named Whitlock and not overwhelmed with humans looking for their fated soul mates. There's nothing in that well for a vampire, except disappointment.

Having resigned himself to a familiar loneliness magnified by the holiday season, Ben is surprised by his attraction to the new fae in town. She reminds him of the sun that he hasn't seen in centuries—bright, shining, and warm.

After sipping from the well and then almost getting hit by a car, Selena decides to give up and leave town. But on her way out, she saves a handsome vampire from being staked. When he offers her a job through the holidays as his bodyguard, she's happy not to spend them alone. But more mishaps plague Selena and the broody vampire that she's trying hard not to fall for.

When all seems lost and the night is at it's bleakest and darkest, Ben and Selena need to put their faith in that magical well one more time in order to save the town, their friends, and perhaps even their hearts' desires.

When Christmas comes around, everyone has their own special wish. For some, those wishes are as simple as getting the perfect gift for that special someone. For others, those wishes are much bigger. Especially, when they wish for love.

Everyone deserves the gift of love, but sometimes that's more complicated than it should be.

This year is different.

For those pure of heart, their wishes, even their wishes for true love, just might be granted.

Wishing for Love is a heartwarming series about Christmas wishes of love coming true for those who have the purest of hearts. If you're looking for a feel-good read this holiday season, pick up A Mistletoe Wish to meet the authors of this heartwarming holiday romance series and find your next happy ever after.

Read more at jamiekschmidt.weebly.com.

Also by Jamie K. Schmidt

Billionaires Behaving Badly
Hard Cover

Christmas Sweeties
The Candy Cane Cowboy
The Gingerbread Cowboy

Hawaii Heat
Life's A Beach
Beach Happens
Beach My Life
Beauty and the Beach

Kennedy Family Christmas
A Casual and Chaotic Christmas Collection
A Second Chance Christmas

Kinky Classics
Domme Quixote

Love Bites
Swipe for Androids

Sons of Babylon
Sentinel's Kiss
Ryder's Reckoning
Necessary Evil: Sons of Babylon MC Romance Book 1
(S.O.B.)

Super Short Super Hero Instalove Romantasy
The Gemini Conflict

The Club Inferno Series
Desire

The Emerging Queens
The Queen's Choice

The Truth & Lies Series
Truth Kills
Truth Reveals

Wishing for Love
A Mistletoe Wish

Standalone
Flash Magic
Naked Truth
Shifter's Price
Maiden Voyage
The Graveyard Shift
Extra Whip
Warden's Woman
Sweet Alchemy: An Explosive Paranormal Romance
Collection
A Casual Christmas
A Chaotic Christmas
A Not So Casual Christmas
Losing It
Dead Man Stalking
Love Bytes

Watch for more at jamiekschmidt.weebly.com.

About the Author

Jamie K. Schmidt is a three-time USA Today Bestseller for her steamy romances *Life's A Beach*, *Heat*, and *The Cowboy's Daughter*. Jamie's books have been called, "hot and sexy, with just the right amount of emotional punch," and "turbo-paced, gritty, highly sexual thrill rides." As a #1 Amazon and Barnes and Noble best seller and a 2018 Romance Writers of America Rita® finalist in erotica, Jamie writes daily, drinks lots of tea, and sneaks away to play video games whenever she makes her deadlines. Along with her husband who lets her stick magnetic signs on his car about her books and her fifteen-year-old son who wants to be her cover model, Jamie lives in Connecticut with her two cats who hate each other and a dog who just wants to be cuddled up on a blanket.

Read more at jamiekschmidt.weebly.com.

9 798223 382997